G000129318

THE DOCKLAND DARLING'S KINDLY ACTS

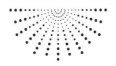

DOLLY PRICE

Publisher's Note: This is a work of fiction. Names, characters, places, and incidents are a product of the author's imagination. Locales and public names are sometimes used for atmospheric purposes. Any resemblance to actual people, living or dead, or to businesses, companies, events, institutions, or locales is completely coincidental.

© 2020 PUREREAD LTD

PUREREAD.COM

CONTENTS

CHRISTMAS PRESENT

1 855

When Clare woke up on Christmas morning and opened her eyes, it took a few moments for her to realise that she was not in her own room. First, she saw the wallpaper. Her own wallpaper was yellow with daisies and bluebells on it, and this wallpaper was blue like the sky, with big red roses. On the wall, she saw a familiar picture—one she liked very much, the lady in red, with the funny veil, on the balcony looking down at a man playing music to her. Romeo and Juliet and the rosy wallpaper belonged in her Grandmama's house in Fernleigh. Waking further, she saw her younger sister Mary sleeping beside her in Grandmama's big four-poster bed that could hold half-a-dozen children. The bedlinen had their grandmother's scent, flowery and faint mothball at the same time.

"Mary! Mary! Wake up! It's Christmas morning! We're in Grandmama's house!" She shook her younger sister.

Mary slowly rubbed her eyes before looking about.

"We went to bed in our own room. And we woke up here!" Clare exclaimed.

"Did Father Christmas put us here?" Mary sounded a little querulous. "Because if we were in a sleigh, with reindeer, why didn't the bells wake us up?"

"I don't know, Mary! If it wasn't Father Christmas, I don't know who brought us here, it must have been the Magic of Christmas."

"What's the Magic of Christmas?"

"Oh, you know, all the grown-up people talk about the Magic of Christmas." Clare slid out of bed and her toes touched the mat on the floor. It was a cold morning, but she did not notice. It was Christmas morning! There was a gaiety and a softness in the morning, and her heart was happy.

"If it wasn't Father Christmas, and he went to our house, and saw we weren't there, would he know to come here?" Mary asked, getting up.

"I don't know. Papa would have left him a note or something."

The white door of the room opened and Aunt Susanna came in, beaming.

"Merry Christmas, children! Are you surprised to wake up in Fernleigh?"

"Did Father Christmas bring us here in his sleigh?" demanded Mary.

"Oh no, he did not, your papa brought you, just after you had fallen asleep last night."

"Why?" demanded Clare, frowning with puzzlement. "Why did he wait until we were asleep?"

Aunt Susanna did not have an answer for that. She just laughed.

"Did Father Christmas come to our house, or did he come here?" asked Clare, now anxious to know if the sudden removal had affected her gifts. "We hung up our stockings on the chimney piece at home!"

"Father Christmas came to your house. And he filled your stockings. Grandmama is at your house now.

After we go to church, I will take you home in a hansom cab."

"We have to wait a long time for our presents, then." Mary said with gloom.

"Now Mary, you know Christmas is not about the presents," lectured Aunt Susanna, but in a very mild tone. "Sadie has a pot of hot milky cocoa brewing, and we'll set off after you have drunk it and eaten some bread and butter. And, by the way, a very special gift arrived at your house at three o'clock this morning."

"What is the very special gift?" Clare asked excitedly.

"A new sister for you."

This caused tremendous excitement, and Aunt Susanna—in getting them dressed, fed and ready to go out—was sorry she had not kept the information to herself until after church, as they did not seem to be able to put themselves to any task, and Mary dropped her bread, butter side down, and made a dreadful mess by squashing it into the polished floor with her heel as she attempted to retrieve it. But never mind. Susanna loved children, and her brother's children were the darlings of her heart.

The girls could hardly sit still in the carriage, and were eager to see the first houses that led into the town of Johns Mills, knowing that they were only a few minutes from home. The hansom drew up outside a modest red-brick terraced house on Raleigh Street, and they tumbled out, pushed open the gate and ran into the house by the back door, which was always open.

"The parlour! The parlour!" cried Clare, leading the way up the back stairs.

"Good morning, girls, and a Merry Christmas," said their father, as they rushed past him. They ignored him.

"Greedy little beasts," he murmured to himself, with a smile.

Their stockings were hanging from a string across the hearth, full to bursting. Clare, at seven years old, could reach them. She took both of them down very gingerly.

"Be careful!" she warned Mary. "She could be in yours."

This brought an even more tender smile to Papa's face, and he watched, saying nothing, as they took out oranges, apples, sweets, nuts, and a rag-doll each. They looked at each other in puzzlement.

"Mama has the new baby upstairs." he said at last, solving the mystery.

The girls hurled themselves past him and up the stairs, making a great clattering.

"Not so much noise! This isn't a bawdy house!" cried Doris, the housemaid, coming downstairs with an armful of linen.

Mama was sitting up in bed, and sure enough, there was a tiny child in her arms, like a little doll, wrapped in a soft pink-and-white blanket. The girls climbed up on the bed and fired a volley of questions.

"What's her name?" "Can she open her eyes?" "When will she wake up?" "Why are you still in bed, Mama?"

"Girls, wait! Wait!" Mrs. Glennon gently passed her hand over the tiny fair head. "Her name is Anna Catherine. Yes, she can open her eyes. She will wake up in a little while, and as for me being in bed, becoming a mama again is very tiring work."

"Can we touch her?"

"Yes, but be very gentle."

"Look, look! She has fingernails!"

"Was I that small, Mama?" asked Mary.

"No, not this small. You were both quite a lot bigger." Their mother's smile faded a little, but the girls did not notice. They were in transports of happiness. Oranges, apples and sweets were remembered in time, of course, but for now, there was just the bliss of being Anna Catherine's big sisters.

Downstairs, the mood was sombre in front of the roaring fire.

"What do you think, Leonard?"

"It could go either way, Sue. I brought her down to the kitchen and weighed her on Cook's scales. Five pounds two ounces wrapped in the blanket. Dr. Langford concurs with me that it depends upon her strength to suck. We'll have her baptised this evening, just in case." He fiddled with an ornament on the tree, a little wrapped sweet.

"With her father a doctor, she cannot do better."

"She cried, so her lungs are healthy. But—there's something else. I fear, from observing her features closely, that the poor child may have—a mental incapacitation. I did not say so to Langford, but I'm sure he noticed it also, but will not aver to it until I do. Many such children do not reach twelve or thirteen years old."

"Oh dear, oh dear." Susanna clasped her hands and unclasped them again. She saw the child's future—slow to walk and talk—unable to learn or play like normal children. People would stare. Some would be unkind. Children would laugh. And then—she would sicken and die. It was very unfortunate.

"What will you do, Leonard?"

"Amanda and I have spoken about it. We are not sending her away. We will keep her here."

"Will you employ a nursemaid for her?"

"We shall see. Amanda thinks not."

Their mother spoke then. She was a woman gentle in demeanour, whose mouth seemed permanently arced in a smile, even in repose, as most of her thoughts were optimistic and pleasant ones. "Anna has a loving family," she said firmly. "For as long as she is here, she will be loved and cherished. Come, let's be cheerful. It is Christmas, and Cook has just checked the turkey—it will be done in an hour or so. We will make merry."

3

DR. & MRS. GLENNON

A year went by, and then two. Anna, as everybody called her, survived, even if she did not grow plump. She had a small, delicate frame and it was always an effort to get her to eat. Her older sisters encouraged her to take steps, and the day she did, three months after her second birthday, was a cause for great celebration.

They tended though, to talk *for* her, until their father forbade them. "Encourage her to talk, girls. Teach her words."

And so they did. They held up dolls, balls, bowls, foods, spoons, everything, and patiently coaxed the words from her. Anna wanted to please them. She loved it when her sisters were happy, and when they whooped for joy when she knew a word, she herself laughed with glee. It did not make any difference to Clare if the word was forgotten the following day— she patiently taught her again. And again.

"Papa, why does she forget things so easily?" Clare remarked to her father one day. "And, Papa, she looks different—from us."

"She's a special child, Clare. She was born with a slowness. She will always need patience and love. And never taunt her about her slowness of mind, or if she cannot do things other children do."

"Papa, of course I wouldn't! I love Anna!"

Anna had the happiest and the calmest nature of all three children. She melted everybody's heart, and everybody knew that her soul would always be pure and angelic. She had straight, fair hair and large, grey eyes. Innocence shone from them.

The older girls' playmates accepted Anna. Clare and Mary were popular with other children, and they saw their devotion to their slower sister. They imitated them in their kind treatment of her. Mrs. Glennon was happy to observe that Anna brought out the caring nature in her daughters and in their friends. Her smiles enchanted adult visitors, even if they went away thanking Providence that they did not have a child with her challenges and difficulties, for if they had, they would not have the courage to raise her with the other children, but hide her away in the servant's quarters.

"She will be made happy for as many years are given her," Mrs. Glennon said to her husband one evening as they sat by the fire. He had come back an hour ago from a sick call to the Wilson family, who lived in a cramped cellar, and was eating a sandwich and drinking tea.

Mrs. Glennon set her cup and saucer back on the tray. Her smile was sweet and sad. "I don't think we should tell Clare and Mary that she may not grow up. It will make them grieve, and I don't want this sword always hanging over them."

"I agree." Dr. Glennon began a second sandwich. *"'Don't ever trouble trouble till trouble troubles you.'"*

Mrs. Glennon nodded. "They love her so much." The fire crackled loudly as the couple thought for a few minutes. Mrs. Glennon broke the silence when her husband reached for another sandwich.

"I think, Leonard, I shocked Cook by cutting the bread as thick as for a ploughman."

"I'm glad you did. I was hungry."

"Clare wants to learn how to cook."

"Clare is interested in learning a different accomplishment every week. What was it last—yes, piano. Thankfully I did not go out and buy her a year's worth of lessons."

"And I think I will put her to this task before she changes her mind again. Even though she will always keep a cook, it's very important that a mistress knows what her cook is doing. This is one interest that I will not allow her to drop. More tea, dear?"

"Mrs. Billings will be afraid to part with her secrets, she may think you have a nefarious plan to replace her."

"I'm not half as afraid of my cook as other women are. Your mother, for instance, lives in constant terror of offending hers and fears she'll be left high and dry an hour before some important guests come."

"Mother has always been terrified of cooks. They only have to say: *'I heard you thought the toast a little too pale this morning, Madam,'* in a very offended, *I'm-giving-notice* tone, and she makes them a gift in appeasement."

"She hates to interview applicants, that is your mother's problem. She never can decide."

"She did not do so badly when she interviewed you for my wife, did she?" Doctor Glennon smiled, helping himself to sugar.

"Oh my, if I had known what she had in mind, I would have run a mile."

"Well my love, thank you for the compliment." They both laughed. Mrs. Glennon had decided that it was time for her son to marry, and she had picked three girls whom she thought suitable, and invited them to tea one-by-one with their mothers. She had fixed upon Amanda Turnbull, and the next time they were invited to Fernleigh, she had contrived for her son to be present. The young doctor and the attorney's daughter had been very attracted to each other, and had fallen in love almost before the third cup of tea. It had gone like a dream.

"Mother prides herself on being a matchmaker."

"I think I caused grave disappointment in the heart of Miss Shelton, though she was never on Mama's list! She liked you."

"But am I not a very handsome man?" He got to his feet and preened in front of the mirror, twirling the corners of his waxed moustache.

"How is it that women are thought to be vain?" asked Amanda playfully. "A man's whiskers are his pride and joy."

"I shall be vain about having the loveliest wife in England instead." He bent to kiss her, but the door opened, and Doris entered to take the tray. Doris was about fifty years old, and had been with the family that had lived in the house before. She was calm and kind, and the children were very fond of her.

"Speaking of your mother—did she ever have anybody in mind for Susanna?" asked Amanda after the door had shut again.

"Susanna was in love once with an officer from India, and nothing came of it; she was not very happy to go so far away. She has never met anybody else she liked."

The conversation lapsed and again, the only sound was the crackling of the fire.

"What was the matter at Wilsons?"

"Typhoid, I'm afraid. The father."

"Will he live?"

"Very doubtful." He sounded grave and matter-of-fact. "He's too thin and weak. The family is living on bread and thin gruel, and not enough of either."

"I will take them some provisions tomorrow. There is a bone from the roast beef, I'll ask Mrs. Billings to make broth."

"I am fortunate to have a charitable and caring wife. But be very careful of contagion."

"I always am, Doctor Glennon. I take soap, and scrub my hands under the pump before I return here, as you advise me. And people laugh at me. What was the name of the woman's doctor in Vienna some years ago who demanded his interns wash their hands after autopsies, before they went to the maternity wards?"

"Dr. Ignaz Semmelweis. A Hungarian by birth. His peers ran him out of Vienna, even though puerperal fever cases dropped dramatically. They were jealous. Pioneers have a difficult time."

4

TRAGEDY

"So Miss Glennon wants to learn to cook," said Mrs. Billings. Miss Glennon was a pleasant girl.

"I knew you would encourage her, Mrs. Billings." Mrs. Glennon beamed. "Every woman should be skilled in cookery and housekeeping. I have heard you say so."

Mrs. Billings could not remember that she had ever said it, but Mrs. Glennon was such a pleasant, cheerful mistress, and she knew a good place when she met it, that she often humoured her.

"Send her down tomorrow, then," she said with the magnanimity that she knew her mistress was looking for. "She can help me make the soup—she will not be averse to chopping onions, I hope, and peeling potatoes."

"Oh no, Mrs. Billings. Get her to do everything. I am very grateful to you."

Happily, this interest in cooking lasted longer than Clare's brief attraction to the piano, and it cost nothing extra, except a bonus to Mrs. Billings from her mistress. At the end of two weeks, Clare was able to make a good thick porridge, and the same in soup; she could prepare vegetables, cook red lentils with an Indian recipe, and had learned the basics of bread making.

"I'm very pleased," beamed Mrs. Billings. "Next week, we'll go on to meats."

But it was not to be. Clare's life altered rapidly on a Sunday evening in the worst way. Her mother and Mary fell very ill. Dr. Glennon diagnosed typhoid fever—the dreaded disease that had killed Prince Albert.

"Papa," cried Clare, seeing her mother unable to lift her head from the pillow. "Will Mama be well soon?"

"Do not come near, Clare. You and Anna must go to Grandmama's house immediately. Doris will take you in a cab."

Anna thought it was a great treat to go to Grandmama's so unexpectedly; she chattered about her ornaments, a set of china figurines inside the glass case.

In Fernleigh, Clare helped Aunt Susanna make up the bed for her and Anna. They laid down the top sheet and a light blanket, followed by the counterpane, and slipped the covers onto the pillows. All this time, Aunt Susanna said nothing. This was very unlike her, and it made Clare uneasy.

Anna was admiring the china figurines in the glass cabinet. They fascinated her. Her favourite was the St. Bernard dog, a shepherd with his flute, and a dancing pair.

"I want to dance!" she always said.

"So you shall, Anna, so you shall." Grandmama always replied, but this time, she seemed rather absent.

The following morning brought Papa. Clare had been watching the window. Dr. Glennon's horse, Pegasus, was all black with a streak of white on his face. She saw the horse from afar, and his rider, and ran downstairs and out to the gate. As soon as he dismounted, Clare's heart dropped. He seemed smaller, hunched. His face was grey and bore long, weary lines.

"I'm sorry to bring you the worst news, Clare. Your dear mother died this morning, and—and Mary—she went only an hour later."

Clare cried out and threw her arms about her father as they walked inside. Grandmama and Susanna came running from the dining room, and Anna, seeing everybody overcome with grief, began to weep also.

The next time Clare saw her beloved mother and sister was when they were laid out in the parlour. A sturdy oaken coffin held Mama, a little white one for Mary.

"This is the end of everything," she thought. "What will Papa do now? How will we go on without her?"

Beside her, Anna was being carried in her Father's arms.

"Papa?" she whispered, pointing. "Dat looks like Mama but Mama not dere. And dat looks like Mary but Mary not dere."

Her father was silent. His heart was full, too full to pay full attention to Anna or to anybody around them. He had been plunged into the greatest affliction.

"Where Mama and Mary?" Anna asked.

"They're in Heaven," said Clare.

"Oh!" Understanding dawned in Anna's large grey eyes. "But dey left dose after dem." She pointed to the remains.

Some mourners suppressed sudden smiles, others thought that this simple-minded girl had more of a grasp of things eternal than many who thought themselves wise and learned.

"They do not need them now," said the rector kindly. "They are in glory."

"Dey do not need now," Anna repeated, in her imperfect articulation. "Dey in glory."

5

NEW SKILLS

"**M**ove in here with us, and let your house," Mrs. Glennon urged her son. "There's plenty of room. The girls will have us to take care of them, and you need not worry about engaging a housekeeper, as you'd surely have to do, if you stay where you are. You'll only be three miles off from your surgery and many of your patients live out this way in any case."

Dr. Glennon was happy to agree. His home at 23 Raleigh Street held painful memories. Clare would soon be at an age when a mother would be needed to inform her of all she needed to know about young womanhood, and Anna needed loving family about her at all times. Her speech and learning was even greater than he had dared to hope for. Her mama and one of her sisters were now gone, but Clare, Aunt Susanna and Grandmama would see to it that she was tended to.

Grandmama and Aunt Susanna tried their best to fill the aching emptiness felt by the loss of Mary and their mother. Aunt Susanna undertook to continue her nieces' education. Clare disliked sitting and learning from books, and wanted to learn how to do things. Sewing was all right, but she had to sit still. She wanted to continue her cookery lessons.

"Oh dear Clare, Mrs. Gerard is a different kettle of fish from Mrs. Billings! She is very particular. But I shall ask your Grandmama."

Surprisingly, Mrs. Gerard was very flattered that one of the 'young misses' wished to learn cookery. She warned that she would be a strict taskmaster, and that Miss Clare would be required to do everything expected of a kitchen maid, except of course, she was only to work two hours in the day and could retire to her soft bed at night instead of to the attic. And *no airs* in the kitchen, if you please. Miss Clare would learn from the most accomplished cook in Devonshire, she told Mrs. Glennon, who wondered quietly why she had wasted herself in the little village of Fernleigh, when her excellent skills could be employed by grand hotels in Plymouth or Exeter.

6

DANCING

M rs. Gerard was as good as her word. Clare was taken aback that on the first day she was given an apron, a mop and a bucket and told to scrub the scullery floor. She complied without a murmur. She decided not to tell her grandmother or Aunt Susanna, they might put a stop to the entire scheme. She loved being in the kitchen more than anywhere else in the house. It was a busy, bustling, stimulating place where something was always happening. It took her mind off her Mama and Mary, and even Papa, who had changed since Mama died. Papa was very quiet and often surly. He went for long walks by himself.

.   .   .

Anna had a very musical ear. Sometimes Aunt Susanna played waltzes on the piano and she would get up and hop and dance around the room. If Aunt Susanna was not about, Anna would hum a waltz to herself as she skipped about. She had never seen a waltz, and did not know that anybody else was involved in it, until she saw the illustration on the cover of a music book. Then she realised that two people should waltz together, the lady in a beautiful dress, and the man smiling at her. She won her father around to dancing with her, and he obliged and was the better for it. He decided that Clare should learn how to dance properly, and so while Susanna played, he guided her around the floor.

7
GOSSIP

"**S**usanna, you have been quiet these last few days. Is there anything the matter?" Mrs. Glennon was mending a petticoat while her daughter was sitting by the window to catch the best light, working a long white lace collar with the aim of refreshing an old gown.

There was a long pause, and finally Susanna spoke.

"Mama, I have been wondering if I should tell you something, and since you ask, I will. Our family seems to be the subject of some talk in the village. I was at Smithson's looking for silk thread and two ladies came in and, while they were waiting to be served, they began to talk with one another, one being Mrs. Bryant, and the other Mrs. Creighton."

"The two biggest gossips in Fernleigh! Go on."

"They did not see me, for I had my back turned and was somewhat bent over the counter examining the threads. Mrs. Bryant said to Mrs. Creighton that she just saw Mrs. Shelton in the street, looking very pleased with the world, and she thought she knew why."

"What? And how could it concern our family?"

"Miss Henrietta Shelton." Susanna pronounced the name slowly.

"What about—what could she possibly have to do with us?"

"I heard Mrs. Creighton say that Dr. Glennon spends almost every evening, if he is not out on a call, with the Sheltons. There, now you have the reason for gossip."

Mrs. Glennon put down her sewing. "Oh no, Susanna. You must be mistaken."

"I'm afraid I am not, Mama. Mrs. Creighton said, quite plainly, that there would be an announcement soon that Miss Henrietta would become engaged to Dr. Glennon."

"Impossible! He would have told us! It's a grave misunderstanding, simply because he whiles away some evenings there, and I'm sure it's just to talk with Mr. Shelton about fishing or boroughs or politics—we must put him on his guard, for he cannot know what kind of expectation he's creating!"

"They seemed to think it a settled thing, Mama."

"Well it cannot be a settled thing, for he has not mentioned it to his mother and sister! We shall put it to him tonight."

"The Sheltons," said Mrs. Glennon, after a pause, "are not our kind."

"I agree, Mama. I think we know how they are different."

"She is pretty, I grant you. She may be trying to draw him in. Surely he knows well enough not to fall for that kind of art and allurement."

"How can he not remember what happened, Mama?"

"He may have forgotten all in his grief and sorrow, and perhaps Miss Shelton, with that bright and spirited air of hers, has driven everything else from his mind. You remember your father, God rest his soul, got the entire story from Dr. Langford because Mr. Davey was his patient. How Mr. and Mrs. Shelton worked on the old man to get him to change his will in their favour, and Mr. Shelton only a cousin! They set him against his own nephew and niece, making them indigent, with no provision made for them at all, while the Sheltons inherited the estate. Now nobody knows where Percy and Caroline are."

There was silence again.

"But, Mama, it could be that Miss Henrietta is not cut from the same cloth as her father. It does not always follow that a bad parent begets a bad child."

"I do not care for Miss Henrietta, Susanna. I don't often speak ill of people, but when she was on the committee to assist the poor inhabitants of Duke Lane after they were flooded out, she showed a distinct hardness of heart. She thought that the homeless families could live in tents, in winter, and not be any the worse for it. There was a poor imbecile boy there by the name of Danny, and she used to mimic him. Many of us were convinced that she was on the Committee simply to be seen, or to exercise power and control over us, as the Sheltons are first in the neighbourhood. It was embarrassing to have her there, and Mrs. Jones, who was President, got rid of her."

Susanna shook her head. "For Leonard's sake, I hope the gossips were wrong. But more than that, for

Clare and Anna's sake. Especially Anna's, who will have to make a permanent home with her. But Mama, how is Miss Shelton interested in Leonard? Johns Mills being only a market town, not of any significance, and Leonard one of the only two hardworking doctors there. We are not a socially prominent family by any means."

"I do not know, Susanna. Nothing is as complex as the affairs of the heart."

8

CONFRONTATION

They heard the front door click, and Leonard let himself in. Anna, as usual, ran to embrace him. Dinner was a quiet affair. Neither mother nor daughter felt like conversing. Anna chattered on in her inarticulate way, for though her vocabulary had very much improved, her speech had not.

Before Leonard left for evening surgery, his mother sent the children out of the room and told him about what Susanna had overheard.

He flushed and looked annoyed, muttered something about women gossiping.

"So it isn't true?" asked his mother eagerly.

"It's not true *yet*," he said. "I'm annoyed that you found out that way; hence my imprecations against the village gossips. I was going to tell you very soon that Henrietta and I are going to become engaged."

A dreadful silence followed.

"You don't sound very congratulatory," he said. "Do you not want my happiness? You're my family, not my Amanda's family, though I hope also that they will be happy for me, and for her children to have a mother again."

In vain his mother remonstrated, reminding him of what her parents had done to Mr. Davey—even mentioning why she had been taken from the committee. Susanna sat in silence, but it was a silence that bespoke disapproval.

"It was not like that at all. Dr. Langford quite misunderstood the matter. Mrs. Shelton has spoken to me of it. She suffered greatly during that time, with everybody judging her and her husband, and few people speaking to her whenever she came into Fernleigh. She does not know why Mr. Davey changed his will to cut his nephew and niece out of it. It has been a source of great anguish to her, and the pair disappeared before they could make any recompense. Now, I don't wish for any more

33

interference in my private affairs, and I am going down to the *Sword & Plough* for some peace."

He left the house angrily and walked briskly to the public house. He wanted to marry again soon. Amanda's loss had left an unbearable gulch, and when he was with Hetty, he felt almost complete again. Almost happy. She was a bright, animated person, her chestnut hair in glossy ringlets about her face, her dark eyes sultry and appealing. These days, he was only happy when he was with her, and she had loved him from afar, for a very long time, he knew.

9

NEW MAMA

"**A**nna, Papa wants to see us." Clare took her sister by the hand and led the way to the parlour.

"He wants to dance with us!" said Anna with delight. "Auntie Susanna!" she called out, for her aunt to come and play music.

But Auntie Susanna did not appear. Papa was sitting by the fire, and beckoned to Anna to sit upon his lap, while Clare sat at his feet.

"I have good news for you," he said. "You are to have a new mother."

"A new movver!" Anna sounded very happy, no doubt having a conviction that the new mother would be exactly like her Mama who was now in Heaven.

The news affected Clare in the completely opposite way. She was appalled—repelled. The thought of a new mother taking the place of dear Mama she found to be impossible—frightful—terrible!

"Papa! You are to be married again!" she said, an expression of ghastly disbelief on her countenance.

"Yes, and it's good news for you both. We will be a proper family again, father, mother and children. Who knows, there may even be little brothers and sisters for you."

"Oh Papa!" Anna hugged him tightly. "Li'l brovers, thister!"

"Well, Clare?" her father had a question in his voice.

"Marry again! How can you, Papa? What about Mama? What about Mama?" Clare got to her feet quickly and ran from the room in a torrent of tears.

"Why's Clare crying, Papa?"

"She misses Mama. But she will get used to the idea. I'm happy you like the idea of a Mama."

"I do, Papa, I do. She will have hair like Mama and thmile and she will dance with me."

"You must not expect her to be like Mama, pet. Not completely. She will teach you, of course. And see that you are clean and fed and happy. Now I must go to Clare." He kissed the top of her head and set her on her feet, where she went dancing from the room to tell Auntie Susanna and Grandmama.

He mounted the stairs and entered his daughter's room where she had thrown herself upon the bed, sobbing bitterly. He sat down next to her.

"Clare, Clare," was all he said at first, as he stroked her hair. "Have your cry-out for Mama. I have, many a time. She is not coming back, and we must get on with our lives. I know I have chosen a good woman, who will do her best to take your mother's place."

Clare continued to weep.

"Oh come, child. It's the beginning of a good new life for all of us," he said a little impatiently. "You must be nice to her, and obey her, and she would be very hurt, I am sure, if she were to see your tears."

Clare went quiet and he left the room. She sat up and wiped her eyes with her handkerchief. Her heart boiled with anger and indignation. Her mother was being replaced! How could her father do that?

10

CHANGE IN THE WIND

The morning was sunny, and Miss Shelton —soon to be Mrs. Glennon—sat in the parlour stitching her wedding gown. The white silk organdie spilled in soft folds and billows over the table. She was sewing buttons on the back, while her mother and her older sister, Mrs. Grant, were sewing seed pearls on the skirt.

"Four weeks more!" said Mrs. Shelton.

Mrs. Grant had arrived only a few hours before, and had not caught all the news.

"What are his family like? Did you meet his daughters?"

"Yes, he introduced me last Sunday. The older one is very plain and surly. The younger—well—the younger." She stopped to bite off some thread.

"What of the younger?"

"You will laugh no doubt. But don't take me for a fool. She's an imbecile."

"OH."

"What do you mean by saying 'OH' like that? Do you think I should not have accepted him because of the daughter?"

"Oh, that is your business. What are your plans for her? Such a child will cause embarrassment when you go to Church every Sunday, and when you have visitors, you shall have to hide her away."

"I shall not have her about me much. I want Dr. Glennon, but that isn't to say I want his children. I will contrive to have Anna sent away. And—her older sister, the surly, plain Clare—off to school with her."

"Have you told their father?" asked Mrs. Grace.

"Oh, not yet. Leonard thinks I will take to mothering them as if they were my own little chicks."

"And let him think that, dear, until you walk down the aisle!" tittered her mother.

"I don't think that's quite right," objected Mrs. Grant. "But if you really can't stand the girls about, and they are too much for you, then he has to accept your feelings. But why is the child not in an asylum already?"

"Because she's been completely spoiled. Everybody panders to her. But it will be a different situation with me."

11

RED FLAG

The first inkling of trouble came with the wedding plans. The occasion was only two weeks away, and Doctor Glennon and Miss Shelton were walking along by the River Ferne, discussing them. Her sister was to be Matron of Honour, and his brother Joseph was coming from Cornwall to stand with him.

"The girls are very much looking forward to the wedding," he said, exaggerating perhaps, because Clare, though she had come around with the help of her grandmother and aunt's cajoling, was still not completely happy. But the promise of a fine new gown to a thirteen-year-old went a good way to throwing the matter into a better light. "Their gowns are all made up, and they insisted upon modelling them for me this morning. Clare's will be this blue creation with a lot of frills and lace, and Anna is enchanted with her gown, which I called pink but which my mother corrected me to call rose. She too has a great deal of lace." He knew that women loved to hear of gowns and lace and thought he had done very well to remember these details.

"Anna?" said his fiancée in a strange, surprised tone. "Anna is to attend?"

"Well of course, my dear." Leonard stopped to face her in some surprise. "Why, did you think she was not to come?"

"Her—em—her health, Leonard. I understood that she was delicate."

"She has a condition which will preclude a long life, but as to her day-to-day health, she is quite robust enough. I am sorry you misunderstood me, Henrietta."

They walked on again, arm in arm.

"She will be capable of the appropriate behaviours for such an occasion … I expect her grandmother and aunt are experienced in managing her." Henrietta said carefully.

"Anna is capable of all social behaviours expected of her. If she slips, it is always in a rather endearing way, such as when I got up to recite a poem at the Annual Lilac Concert last year. As I was making my way to the stage, Anna turned around in her chair to everybody in the hall and with a very proud and delighted face, I was later told, pointed toward me and mouthed the words: *'That's my Papa!'* to the audience. Everybody was charmed! My dear Hetty, you will need to get to know my youngest daughter a great deal better."

"That sounds like a reproach, Leonard. I heard it in your voice." Henrietta's tone was injured and clipped.

"Oh my dear Hetty. Not so." He patted her arm and looked at her anxiously. They walked on again, but she said little. She seemed to be in a bad mood. He thought it an odd thing, but put it down to pre-wedding nerves. For a woman, marriage brought so much that was new and perhaps alarming. And she would have to settle into his home, the home that had had another mistress, a beloved mistress at that, and she would become an instant mother.

Her mood did not improve as they neared her home. She left him with a cool *'good evening.'* He made his way home, pondering, with an uneasiness stirring in his breast.

She doesn't like Anna.

No, he corrected himself, *she does not know Anna. It was impossible for any person not to like my daughter Anna!*

The following evening, after surgery, he called into her home to see her. She was all smiles, happy and warm and embraced him and they kissed, and he pushed the misgivings he had felt to one side.

In years to come, he would bitterly regret not probing her character a little deeper and finding the truth about her feelings with regard to his youngest daughter.

12

CAPTAIN HAMMOND

The girls stayed on with their Grandmama and Aunt Susanna while their father took his new bride to Weymouth for two weeks. The weather was sunny and they played out in the garden, and one day, while batting a shuttlecock about, they saw a cab stop outside the gate. A gentleman alighted from it in a tall black hat and a smart red jacket decorated with broad ribbon and epaulets. He did not see them, so intent was he upon taking a survey of the house, as if pondering. Then with a quick, determined stride he opened the squeaking gate and walked up to the front door.

Both girls were awed by the bright, smart uniform. They crept up almost beside him, hiding themselves behind a white rhododendron bush, until the housemaid opened the door.

"Sadie!" the visitor said in a hearty voice. "Do you recognise me?"

"Captain Hammond!" Sadie gasped after a moment. "After all this time! Oh, you do look very fine!" She gave a quick curtsy and let him in.

Their shuttlecock was forgotten, and they went around to the back of the house and in the kitchen door, and heard Sadie say: "And of course it's Miss Glennon he has come to see! You should've seen her when I told her who was come! She turned pale at first, and then blushed like a rose! She hasn't forgotten him at all!"

This was met with titters until the girls appeared, making their way through the kitchen and taking the back stairs up to the parlour where visitors were entertained. Clare pushed open the door quietly with Anna upon her heels, and both girls seated themselves primly upon the small sofa along the wall inside the door, where they had a good view of all that was going on.

Captain Hammond was seated in the best chair by the chimney-piece. He was a handsome man, and having removed his hat, was seen to have straight brownish hair. His eyes were blue and took on a soft, almost silly look when they turned toward Aunt Susanna. Grandmama was in the chair opposite the Captain and was asking a great deal of questions about India and Lancers and the mutiny and the climate. Aunt Susanna seemed more quiet than usual but she laughed when the Captain made a joke, and the few times she spoke, it was in a sort of breathless manner.

Grandmama, at last perceiving the girls, introduced them. The Captain rose to his feet and bowed. Clare was very impressed. He stayed to tea, and she observed him and Aunt Susanna. The way they looked at each other was so tender and romantic! She looked very nice indeed, and had put on her pretty lace barege shawl.

Over the next two weeks they saw a great deal of Captain Hammond. He was in England for six months and Clare waited impatiently for the inevitable engagement. He stayed at the Sword & Plough and called every day and took them all out on walks, but always walked with Susanna. They went for a picnic by the river, and Clare saw them holding hands. Her heart soared, and her romantic imagination leaped. Would there ever be a Captain Hammond for her? When she looked in the mirror sometimes, she was tempted to doubt. She was not beautiful, not like Jenny Tighe who had a pretty nose or Katharine Holmes whose eyes were framed by long dark eyelashes.

NEWLYWEDS

T he newlyweds returned from Weymouth to the news that Susanna was head over heels in love and that they would surely lose her to this handsome officer.

"Is he to apply to me or to you for her hand, Mama?" asked Dr. Glennon in an intrigued, amused tone as they drank tea in the parlour. "And should I give my blessing?"

"If it is what she wants, to marry and go back to India with him, then I will not stand in her way," said his mother, but with a sad little sigh. "He is in every respect the kind of man I would wish for Susanna. If only his regiment would return to England, it would all be perfect."

The new Mrs. Glennon was thinking of other matters.

"Mother Glennon, I would be so obliged to you if you could keep the girls for another four weeks or so, to give me a little time to organise the house, for with tenants having been there for quite some time, it may be in need of some redecorating, and other preparations."

"But I have sent Sadie and Tom over there to get everything ready," Mrs. Glennon replied, after a pause resulting from the unexpected sobriquet, which had put *Mother Goose* into her head. "The servants are re-engaged; all is prepared. But if you would appreciate a little time to settle in before you take on the duties of mother, I shall be happy to keep them for another while."

"I am obliged to you, Mother Glennon." The younger woman buttered a scone and took a bite. "Superior baking! Your cook has a light hand."

"The scones were baked by Clare especially for Papa and Mama," smiled the proud grandmother. "She's such an active girl. Always busy, and can't bear to sit for any length of time. Anna helped her, mixing the ingredients and kneading the dough."

"I'm afraid I am helpless in the kitchen. Mama kept a very skilled cook."

"As we did, my dear, but Clare wished to learn," her husband put in.

"I daresay she may teach me in that case," was the somewhat pert quip, as she took another bite.

The acid tone did not escape Mrs. Glennon. Out of the corner of her eye she glimpsed her son. Had she seen his lips tighten, just a hint?

She had also observed the cool manner of the new Mrs. Glennon toward little Anna. The latter, in her exuberant manner, had thrown herself into her father's arms in greeting and been lifted up for a kiss. A moment later Anna had been set upon the floor again and had turned with open arms toward her new mother. But Hetty, almost as if in anticipation of this, had already turned away from her and was admiring Clare's hair-ribbons.

Perhaps Hetty should be given the benefit of the doubt. Perhaps she had overlooked Anna unintentionally. But she had forgotten—or intentionally ignored—the child since she had arrived.

EVIL WIND

Ore day about three weeks later, a fine carriage drawn by four horses drew up outside the Glennon house in Fernleigh, and the new Mrs. Glennon was seen to alight, accompanied by her father, Mr. Shelton.

"My father has offered his carriage to take the girls home," she said brightly.

"Oh! But we were not expecting—" said her mother-in-law.

"Oh, Mother Glennon, it is a good opportunity! By the way, Leonard is gone away for a week. After we returned home, he found a letter inviting him to a conference in Bristol this week. I thought it an ideal opportunity for me to fetch the girls and surprise him upon his return. Is it not a good plan?"

Put like that, neither Grandmama nor Aunt Susanna could think of an objection, though they bridled at the short notice. They fetched the girls in from the garden, packed their boxes and told them they were going home at last.

Neither girl was happy to see that their Papa was not of the party. Anna wept as she embraced her grandmother and aunt. But the false promise (from her stepmother) that her father awaited her at home cheered her.

"Mama," said Clare, though the name was strange and wrong on her tongue. "Grandmama said that Papa was away."

"And so he is, but he will be back," said Hetty brightly.

Clare remembered the journey they had made that Christmas when Anna was born, how she and Mary had eagerly looked out for signs that they were nearing Johns Mills. Now she was not so cheerful.

At Raleigh Street, they felt like visitors instead of the children of the house. Mr. Shelton left for his home again and they were alone with their new mother.

"Did you not enjoy that fine carriage?" said Mama. "You shall tell your father all about it. Now come into the back parlour, I wish to speak with you."

As they sat uneasily there, with many objects reminding Clare of her mother, their new Mama stood before them. He face had taken a stern look, and Anna shrank a little and moved toward her older sister.

"Your father is a very busy doctor," she said "And you are not to bother him with any problems you have. You are to come to me. Now, your rooms—" she went on, while Clare looked uneasily at her. "I understand that you have always shared a room, but that will not be the case anymore. Clare, you will have the room you always had, and Anna will have the room above it."

"But that's an old attic!" Clare cried out, jumping up.

"Sit down, Clare. It's a perfectly good room."

"Why cannot Anna have one of the other rooms? There are two more, and one has a lovely view of the bird bath in the back—Anna loves little birds!"

"I have taken the back room as my own. The other will be a guest room, always ready for the unexpected visitor. My family is a large one and they will come to visit. Now do not complain. What are you saying? I don't understand a word!" She looked in an annoyed way at Anna, who had begun to talk quickly, so quickly that she sounded high-pitched and unintelligible.

"Anna is saying that she wants to sleep in the same room as me," Clare said, putting an arm around her sister. "She's never slept on her own before. Please."

"She's quite old enough to sleep in her own room now! And you Clare, growing into a young woman, should be very grateful that you are being given a room of your own! I never had that luxury. Now there is to be no more about it. Come with me."

She led the way upstairs, and placed Clare in her room to unpack and settle in. Clare heard her take Anna up to the attic, where she left her, shutting the door. She heard her go downstairs again.

In a trice, Anna came down to Clare's room, crying. She sobbed over and over that she didn't want to sleep on her own, she was frightened. She was sure there were spiders under the bed!

Upon her entreaties, Clare went up to check for spiders. The room itself was a tiny servant's room, with a bare floor, and no fireplace. The bed was an old narrow iron bedstead with a straw mattress, and there was nothing of cheer there, only old faded window-curtains upon the window high up, and peeling walls. An old wardrobe stood in the corner. Clare looked around at it with distaste. What was her stepmother thinking of, to give Anna a room like this?

Clare got down on her stomach and peered under the bed.

"There are no spiders here, Anna," she reassured her.

"Why doesn't Mama like me?" Anna sobbed. "I'll tell Papa, I will!"

Clare did not know what to say. She sat on the bed and comforted her.

Downstairs in the kitchen, Doris was angry. "It's not right that a child should be put up there! I tole her, when she ordered me to go and clear out the room and make up the bed, that I worked in this house when the last family, the Dobsons, were here, and nobody has ever slept in that room; it was always considered too cold and draughty, even when I was scullery maid here, it was only considered fit for storage, I said *'and begging your pardon, but that's not fit for an animal to be put in'* She got angry and tole me to hold my tongue. I was so angry I slammed the door, and she called me back and asked if I'd like to be put out on the street, and I said '*I'm very sorry, Madam.*' But she knew I din't mean a word of it. I'm giving in my notice. You know what I think? She wants us to give notice! She wants to bring her own servants in, what do you bet but that she has promised them a good wage here in the town? She's gone out of her way to annoy and vex me, and I don't know about you, Mrs. Billings, but I'll be off next Monday fortnight."

"She questioned my accounts." Mrs. Billings said. "I'm paying too much everywhere, the greengrocers, the bakers, the butchers. She wants me to patronise the other butcher. But I've a good understanding with Mr. Harold and he saves exactly the cuts that I like. Poor Mrs. Glennon! The last one I mean, the good, kind woman. We had our differences but she respected my work. She respected it as mine and she knew she could trust me. This harridan does not. I'm giving notice too. Mrs. Langford's cook is retiring, and you'll see if I don't get her place!"

"Doctor Glennon has gone and made a terrible mistake, and that's what I say," added Doris, in tones more hushed. "Drat it all, is that the bell again? What does she want now?"

THE LITTLE CHAT

When Clare had put away her clothes and helped Anna with hers, they went downstairs and out into the garden. Anna was still upset and tearful, and Clare tried to distract her by throwing the shuttlecock about.

The front door opened, and Mama stood there. She looked rather angry.

"Come inside directly," she said. "Anna, you go back up to your room. Clare, I have some sewing for you to do. Who told you that you could go out and play whenever you like? Do you never ask permission to do anything? Anna!" she shouted, as the girl had not moved an inch. "Did you not hear me? Go to your room and stay there until I say so! Go on, go, before I get even more angry."

Anna ran inside, terrified.

Clare was very afraid also. They had only been home for two hours, and already they felt as if they were in a prison. She meekly followed her stepmother into the back parlour.

"Sit down, Clare. I have to talk to you."

Her tone was softer, but it did not reassure Clare, she could hear the sobs from the attic coming through the house.

"Now Clare, my dear, if I may call you that. I want to be your friend. I know I cannot take the place of your mother. She apparently was a saint. I see tears in your eyes, very natural. You wonder why I'm being hard with Anna, I suppose. You have a natural affection for her, and that's to your credit. But people like Anna must learn that they do not belong in society. No, do not interrupt me. I will tell you why. Anna is slow. Very, very slow. She does not look like you or me, you see her odd features—she is abnormal, is she not? Well, is she not?"

"She is my sister," said Clare evenly, jumping up.

"Sit down! I can't stand your restlessness. But we will speak of that at another time. Something has to be done about Anna, and I have a plan. You must support me in my application to your father."

Clare felt all the injustice, the outrage of this.

"Would Anna not be happier to be among her own kind?" her stepmother asked.

"What do you mean?"

"Among people like her. She could be with them, you know, and nobody would remark her, or laugh at her, or laugh at us."

"People have never laughed at us!"

"Oh, not to your face, of course. But behind your back, you can be sure of it."

Clare remembered some staring, and yes, some derision from children when they were out in public. But in general, people were kind.

"Clare, do you want to get married some day?" her stepmother asked unexpectedly.

Clare blushed, and felt a little shy at this discovery of her secret wish. She was very young, she knew, but to have someone feel for her as the Captain felt for Aunt Susanna—that she wanted—someday—a long time off, of course. She dreamed of a dashing, handsome officer such as he was.

"Well, do you?"

"I suppose so," was Clare's coy answer.

"There's no need to be bashful about it. Every girl wants to fall in love. But in order to be attractive to the opposite sex, some things are necessary, and one of those things is that every man wants to marry a girl whose family is healthy."

"My mother and sister died of typhoid."

"That's different. They caught a disease. Anna, however, is not normal. A man would be afraid that *her condition runs in the family*. So people with somebody like Anna often send their loved ones to institutions to be cared for. It's the best thing for everybody. And they have a wonderful time there, with their own kind, and not a care in the world, for they do not have to do any work, but eat and sleep as much as they wish, and go into the gardens and sit there. What a lovely life!"

"I don't know what you're talking of, Mother." The word Mama would not come out. Mama was good, loving and nice, this woman was a false Mama.

"Of course, you do," said her stepmother in a coaxing way. "There is a building at the edge of town, full of people like Anna. *The Asylum*. She should go there, Clare, and then you could be free to get on with your life, and have your education, and have every advantage, and marry well."

Clare was shocked beyond belief. She felt that this was the most unfair, horrid thing she had ever heard of!

"You need every advantage you can find, Clare. I speak as a friend. You will have trouble filling your dance cards; you are not pretty. Anna will hold you back even further. Will you support me, when I bring the matter up with your father?"

But Clare had stopped listening. If there is a sure way to incur the bad opinion of a thirteen-year-old girl, it is to tell her that she is not pretty. Clare stared down at her lap for a moment; she knew she was plain, she often sighed about it, and here was confirmation. Her brow was too high for beauty. Her nose was too long. Her mouth was too wide, and worst of all, she had freckles! But she had thought that a man would fall in love with her someday. There was a young man somewhere out there in the world, in the misty future, who would think her more beautiful than every other girl in the world! Tears came to her eyes.

"I wish my father had never married you!" she burst out, jumping up and running for the door, her hair flying behind her. "And—why do you need the back bedroom in any case? My own Mama and Papa slept in the same room!"

"Well, well! What an impudent, wild creature you are! There's gratitude for you! I am trying to be a good mother to you, and advise you! You go to your room and think very hard about what I said!"

She went instead to Anna's room and comforted her.

Dinner was at six o'clock. Anna was not allowed to sit at the table, instead a meal was brought to her room on a tray. Her stepmother talked again of the asylum, until Clare said:

"Papa will never put Anna into that place. He hates it! He has some patients in there, and I've heard him say that mentally deficient people such as our Anna for instance, should not be there, in with insane adults. *So there.*"

Her stepmother was silent for the remainder of the meal. Afterward, she made Clare sit and sew. The rest of the evening was spent in a kind of unreal horror. Before she went to bed, Clare went to Anna's room, but the door was locked. This was very puzzling! Had she locked herself in? She knocked quietly—no reply. Uneasy, she did not know what to do. She stole down to the kitchen and asked Doris why the door was locked.

"I don't know why, but Madam had a new lock put in. She has the only key."

"Why is Anna so quiet, Doris? I'm worried that she's all right."

"She got something to make her sleep." Doris clenched her lips shut.

"I think, Miss Clare, that you should write to your Grandmama," said Mrs. Billings quietly. "As for us, we're about to hand in our notice."

"Oh, don't go!" Clare burst out. "Wait until Papa gets home! Everything will be put right then!"

"Clare?" Mrs. Glennon appeared in the kitchen. "Did I not tell you that you must not roam about the house without telling me where you are going?"

Clare turned on her heel and followed her stepmother up the stairs.

CRISIS

The atmosphere in Fernleigh was happy the following morning. Susanna received a letter from Captain Hammond, who had had to go to Exeter for a few days. He wrote of his love and she knew to expect a proposal upon his return. At breakfast, she coyly said so to her Mama, who had now accepted that Susanna would leave her for Hammond and for India, and with the sacrifice many mothers are used to making, concealed her own grief very well and murmured words of congratulation and delight.

Sadie entered the room.

"Excuse me, Ma'am. There's a servant from Johns Mills here to see you urgently. It's Doris Parkinson. Shall I send her up, Ma'am?"

"Doris! Of course!" Mrs. Glennon looked at Susanna in anxiety. "There's something the matter. She bears a message about Leonard! He has been in an accident—or perhaps one of the girls is ill!"

"Mama, wait. Don't be so anxious."

Doris was shown in. "You bear us bad news, Doris, do you not? Out with it—what is it? What has happened?"

"It's Miss Anna, Madam. She is in a very bad way. Very bad. The new Mrs. Glennon has locked her into the attic room—you know, the one that was used to store things—and she's in there crying her heart out, terrified. She's been in there nearly a day now, since she returned yesterday."

"Why? Why would Mrs. Glennon lock her up?"

"You see, Madam, that's her room now, upon Mrs. Glennon's orders. She is to sleep there. And eat there. And this morning when I brought up her breakfast, I found her crouched in the corner, shivering with cold, and weeping."

An awful silence descended on the parlour.

"Her bed was wet, Madam. And little Miss Anna hasn't wet her bed for a long time. Not since she was four, I'm sure. I din't make a fuss, Madam, and was cheerful, telling her not to mind it—and urging her to have some hot porridge—" here, Doris broke down. "—I took the wet sheets off and was trying to get them downstairs unbeknownst—but *she* caught me, and I had to tell her. And so she went upstairs—and she struck her."

"Struck Anna! But where was Clare?"

"At the foot of the stairs, crumpled in a heap, screaming and crying. She is in a bad way too. So I spoke to Mrs. Billings, and she said *'get yourself out to Fernleigh quick as ever you can!'* I took the liberty of taking a hansom, and he's waiting outside, Madam. She will have missed me, I'm sure, but I gave notice yesterday, and I don't care if I never—"

"We must go directly," said Susanna. "Oh mother, poor little Anna! What will Leonard say when he returns?"

Within an hour, they were in the house, taken in the back way by Doris.

"Mother Glennon and Susanna! You quite surprised me!" said Hetty. She was sewing in the back parlour with Clare, who looked up, her red tear-streaked face alive with hope.

"Give me the key to the attic," said Susanna, holding out her hand.

Hetty looked discomfited. She went pale and trembled a little as she fished in her pocket and brought forward the key.

"I did not mean any harm!" she cried as they ascended the stairs. Clare had thrown down her sampler and was following them.

They left a short time later with Clare and Anna. Hetty took out her paper and pen, and wrote a letter.

Dearest Leonard, please do not be alarmed, but I must tell you what is passing here in your absence. I thought to get the girls back to surprise you upon your return, but a series of misunderstandings happened, and your mother and Susanna came to Johns Mills (upon the word of a servant!) and bore them away again. Doris completely misunderstood the situation and she acted upon her own. Needless to say, she will be dismissed without a character. I will tell you the full story when you arrive home, but please do not be anxious, all is well _now_. I miss you so much, my love, and want you back as soon as possible. And—though it is too early to be sure—there is reason to suspect that a little stranger may be upon the way! I can hardly wait to see you, my darling. Your loving wife,

Hetty. p.s. Clare is a sweet girl, and we are friends already. She will be a credit to you.

She sent the letter in the mail and waited anxiously for a reply, which came two days later.

Dear Hetty, your letter contained hopeful and disconcerting news. You need to wait a little longer, my dear, to be of the opinion that a child may be on the way— but if it be true, then I rejoice. As for the other happening —I am surprised at Doris, she was always highly thought of, and whatever occurred must have been completely misconstrued! You can tell me all about it when I return. I also have much to tell you, but suffice it to say that this has been a very informative conference for me professionally and personally—I had the great fortune to be introduced to Dr. John Langdon Down, a West Country man like me but who now practises in Surrey, who is very interested in children like our Anna. We had a very good conversation. He is of the opinion, which I concur with, that children like Anna are capable of so much more than society—or even many physicians—give them credit for. My darling, I will rely upon you to set our Anna upon a meaningful, and meritorious path with crafts or drawing or something in that line. I told him of her love for dancing and how it has helped her balance, etc. But we will speak more of this when I return. I hope you are right about our little stranger, but if not, we have been only married six weeks! All my love, Leonard.

This was not a satisfactory reply. She crumpled the paper and threw it into the fire. She was not with child, but she wished only to distract him.

She was sorry she had acted as she did now. It was wrong, but her mother had told her to begin as she meant to go on, and she did not want Anna to be part of her life. Most idiot children lived with the servants and were raised by them. But this family had done it differently, and led Anna to believe that she was one of them. She could never allow that, never.

Perhaps Anna would stay with her grandmother. Yes, that would be a good solution. And Clare? Clare had to go away to school, and soon. She did not want Clare about her. It would be easy to persuade Leonard to send her, she needed refinement and polish, and to learn French and drawing, and to return, at seventeen or so, ready for marriage.

17

DR. GLENNON'S RETURN

Hetty awaited her husband's return with some anxiety. She watched for him on Saturday afternoon through the front parlour window. The rain kept up a steady patter when he at last put his key in the lock and let himself in. She rushed to greet him. There was a warm, loving embrace in the Hall before she helped him off with his hat and coat and put away his umbrella in the rack.

Dinner was brought to the table by a housemaid strange to him.

"A new face, I see," remarked Dr. Glennon.

"Yes, this is Gertie."

"Welcome, Gertie. I hope you are happy here and settle in before long."

"Oh I'm already settled, Dr. Glennon, for my sister is housemaid at Sheltons, so I'm well acquainted with the mistress already, as I used to help out sometimes when they had visitors." She set a bowl of stew upon the table, curtsied, and left.

Hetty ladled some of the aromatic mutton stew onto her husband's plate.

"So, Hetty my love, are you going to tell me of the misunderstanding?" he asked after they had talked of some other matters.

She gave him the story she had prepared—very simply that Anna had thrown a severe fit and she, Hetty, had become frightened, and thought Anna would harm herself so she put her in the attic (she was sure that the attic would be mentioned by Mother Glennon) out of sight because Clare was distressed. (She hoped that Clare would not be asked for her version of events). She regretted her action now, if she had foreseen that Anna would be affrighted by it, she would not have done it at all.

To her dismay, her explanation did not go over with Leonard. He stared at her, a puzzled frown upon his brow.

"A fit? What kind of fit? A seizure? That has never happened to her before. And which attic—not the storage attic—what? That one? I don't understand you."

"I erred in placing her there. It was a severe fit—and Doris decided, of her own volition, to fetch your mother and Susanna, without as much as a word to me. No doubt she was affrighted, but there was no call to act like that—Anna was safe, and I was just by the door."

"She was alone in the attic while she was having a seizure?"

"Yes—well—no. I was by. Very close by."

Hetty hoped that he would not demand the story from his mother-in-law and that she, in turn would not reveal much. Families had to use a great deal of discretion to avoid driving a wedge between a husband and wife. She would rely on that.

"Hetty, I still do not see the necessity for taking Anna up to the attic. Did you carry her up while she was seizing?"

"Well, yes. I did."

"That does not make sense, Hetty. Why did you do that, instead of setting her upon a sofa—and you would have passed her own room on the way to the attic! Where was she when she seized?"

"Really, Leonard—this is beginning to sound like an interrogation!"

"I only wish to know exactly what happened. Did you carry her up while she was seizing?"

She refused to answer. There was a dreadful silence. He ate his dinner and she offered him more, but he waved away her hand. He seemed to be simmering with anger. At last he spoke.

"The matter I spoke of in my letter—my meeting with Dr. Down—did you think it a good thing?"

"I'm sure I don't know him," was her icy reply.

"Anna needs special attention."

"She cannot get such from me, Leonard. I am not the person."

"I am disappointed, Hetty," he said stiffly. "You knew, before you married me, that Anna was a part of our household. Other families may hide their abnormal children, or put them away, we decided not to."

"'*We*'!" she repeated. "'*We*'! I am not the first Mrs. Glennon, Saint Amanda the Patient. Anna's not my child. I have no affection for her. She is an idiot child. I feel it incumbent upon you to consider my feelings. Everybody else sends those children away."

"And I have seen where they send them away to, Mrs. Glennon," he said with anger. "Atrocious conditions, punishments, restrained hand and foot—nothing to do but stare at the walls all the day long—my daughter is worth more to me than that!"

She got up and stormed from the room. But before she left, she said,

"Clare is to go to school. I insist upon it."

"I say, Hetty, was there any necessity to dismiss Doris?" he shouted in turn.

"The servants are my affair, Leonard." she said in a taut tone. "She was impudent. She's gone. And—Mrs. Billings has heard of a situation that suits her better—she's leaving the end of next week. But I have engaged a cook."

"A relative I suppose?" he countered in a withering tone.

She slammed the door. He was left to look out at the pouring rain outside the window. Lightening flashed, followed by a thunderclap.

He would have to ask his mother to take Anna permanently. If they could find Doris, he would re-engage her to help his mother. Doris loved Anna and Anna loved Doris. And Clare—yes, school for Clare! He would not have his older daughter under the influence of her stepmother—she'd lied and lied. He knew it.

As for his own happiness in the conjugal state—at this moment, he felt that it had all evaporated. What a bitter quarrel, only weeks after the wedding!

He remembered a piece of advice, *do not let the sun go down on your anger*. After fighting with it for a bit, he tried his wife's bedroom door on his way to bed. She had not locked it as he feared. She bid him come to her, but he said, "goodnight, we shall speak tomorrow," and retired to his own room. They had to live with each other forever, and could not be enemies. But let her wait a while for full forgiveness!

18

MASTER EDGAR

"Excuse me, Madam."

Mrs. Murgatroyd looked up from her carpet-work. She'd just begun it, her threads were all arranged, and she was annoyed.

"What is it, Pringle?"

"It's the tradesmen again, Madam. They won't go away without seeing you."

"But that's ridiculous. It's not me they have to see, it's my husband."

Pringle suppressed a sigh.

"They are not going away, Madam."

"All right, all right, I hear them, like the mobs in Paris."

In recent days, Mrs. Murgatroyd had become preoccupied with Queen Marie Antoinette, her favourite dead queen in history. Her grandmother, Aidah Mountchurch, had seen her once in Paris. She named her daughter Marie Antoinette, who had named her daughter Aidah Marie Antoinette. Some thought it an unfortunate name to carry about, but Aidah Longfellow wore it with great pride, grew up vivacious and pretty, fell in love with and married an ambitious man named Reginald Murgatroyd, and had produced a son, whom she wanted to call Louis but who her husband insisted on naming Edgar after his father. The child received his mother's maiden name.

"They're making a lot of noise, Mother," Edgar said. It was the school holidays and he had just come in from a ramble in the woods around his Oxfordshire home with his friend Timothy. He ran upstairs and came down again with his box under his arm. Edgar had a coin collection.

At twelve years old, he was tall for his age and interested in old coins. His mother did not understand his interest; she thought it more befitting an eccentric gentleman of reclusive habits. She did not want him to turn out like her uncle.

Uncle Evelyn had never seen Edgar but sent him an old coin every Christmas, for which he was dutifully thanked by him in a polite letter. But Edgar was no recluse, nor was he a retiring boy, for as well as coin-collecting, he liked to roam the fields with his friends and annoy angry farmers and bulls, both from a safe distance, of course.

At school he played rugby, was doing well in the Classics and would surely follow his father into politics. Though Mr. Murgatroyd's bid for a seat in the House of Commons had failed, Mrs. Murgatroyd was sure that Edgar would be successful.

After some time, the tradesmen went away—they always did. Edgar, like his mother, simply thought they were there to make trouble for them.

"

EDGAR'S PLANS

It was late, and Mr. Murgatroyd had not returned. Edgar was taking rubbings from an ancient Greek coin with a pencil.

"I think, Mother, I would like to become an archaeologist," he said quite seriously. "I would like nothing better than to dig at an old Roman site and see what I could find. Just think of all the coins the Romans dropped all over England!"

"My dear boy, that's no occupation for a gentleman!" Mrs. Murgatroyd was put immediately in mind of Egyptologist James Burton, who was notorious for opium and women, and who had brought a female slave from Greece to England and wed her, causing his family to disown him.

"But they are all gentlemen, Mama. Otherwise their parents would make them stick at a boring occupation like law or something."

"You must learn how to play at cards. You will not have many friends if you don't know how to play backgammon or poker."

"King Louis the Fourteenth collected coins," Edgar said, knowing his mother's weakness for Royalty.

"Did he, really? How do you know?"

"Father told me."

"Where is your father? It's past nine o'clock. Time for bed, Edgar. Put those away."

"May I not stay up until he comes back?"

"No, put them away now."

Edgar sighed and put them away as slowly as he could.

"Goodnight, Mother." He offered her his cheek for a kiss.

"Goodnight, Edgar. Don't read in bed. You'll ruin your eyes."

Another pastime closed to him tonight! Parents not only spoiled the fun they saw you having, they also spoiled the fun you were going to have out of their sight, which, Edgar reflected as he mounted the stairs, was not fair. How did they even know you *might* read in bed?

He had just reached his room when he heard his father's key in the front door. The butler, having heard it also, came forward to take his hat and coat.

"How are you, sir?"

"Not good. Is Mrs. Murgatroyd up?"

"She is in the drawing room, sir."

Before he reached the top of the stairs, Edgar heard his mother cry out.

19

UNCLE EVELYN

He wondered what was afoot. Perhaps Uncle Evelyn in London had died and left them all his money. Edgar had never known his great-uncle but had a slight fondness for the uncle who sent him a gift every Christmas. His parents had been expecting Uncle Evelyn to die for months now, maybe years. They never said they were looking forward to it but he supposed they must be, as they constantly alluded to it, and occasionally threw in that he had pots of money. It usually went like this:

'Any news of your granduncle, my dear?' 'Oh he is worse, Reggie, much worse.' 'I am sorry to hear of it, Aidah.' Newspaper rattle. 'But I suppose it must be his time soon. What age is he, again? Eighty-four? Most men of his age are gone six foot under.' (said resentfully) 'His housekeeper

thinks the Scotch is keeping him alive, Reggie, for he eats nothing.' 'As long as he isn't eating his bags of sovereigns, Aidah. For we could use them here, in due course.' 'If he eats nothing, depend upon it, Reggie, he won't last till Christmas/Easter/Midsummers/Michaelmas.' Subject forgotten for about six weeks, then it was repeated.

This time, Uncle Evelyn might have died. He put on a rather sorrowful face as expected of a grieving relative as he entered the breakfast-room.

"Good morning, Father," he said with gloom. "Good morning, Mother." He sat down.

He expected his parents to give him the news, but his mother continued to butter her toast, muttering that the edges were burnt, and his father read the newspaper.

"Any news, sir?" asked Edgar.

"Price of cotton gone up again." This was directed toward his wife. She raised her head and then Edgar knew what the cry last night had been about—she'd been defending herself again against an accusation of extravagance. After all, his father had said numerous times to his wife in the past several years *'You'll bankrupt me, if you go on like this!'*

"Well I'm sure I have not bought any cotton of late," she defended herself.

"Not cotton maybe, but what about that satin gown, and new furniture for your boudoir? We have to retrench, Aidah."

"What's retrench?" asked Edgar, cutting an apple. His mother would not allow him to eat it at the table as he ate it in the orchard.

"It means that your father thinks I'm spending too much money. He has his cigars, though, and his beaver hats. *He* won't go without."

Edgar sensed a quarrel brewing, so he asked brightly, "Any news of Uncle Evelyn?"

"Uncle Evelyn! What put Uncle Evelyn into your head?" asked his mother in astonishment.

"You said he might leave us his money," Edgar replied defensively, between munching the apple quarters.

"I never said any such thing," said his mother, affronted.

"Nor did I," said his father hastily. "Mercenary little son we have, Mrs. Murgatroyd."

Edgar sighed. "But you often ask about him," he pointed out, whereupon each parent told him in a chorus to be quiet and they changed the subject.

Edgar walked over to his friend Timothy after breakfast. They grumbled about the oddities of parents before they climbed trees and had a jolly morning.

20

TRAGEDY

e returned home for lunch in time to see a large cart draw up outside the door. The men lifted what looked like a table and chairs out of it, but covered as they were with cloth, he could not be sure. His mother was going to be in more trouble later with his father! He sauntered into the house to see his mother direct the men to place them into the dining-room. She was flustered and gesticulating in a rapid way. The men were apparently doing everything wrong.

"Not there! By the window! No, not that near to the window. Move it out a bit."

"Ma'am, our orders are to deliver 'em, not to arrange 'em to anybody's perticler fancy," said the man who was evidently in charge of the operation. "Our duty is as done when they was on your doorstep, and it's only out of the kindness of my 'eart that we brought them in further."

"What impudence! I shall see that you're dismissed!"

"Who's going to dismiss me, Madam? I owns the cart."

"Then I shall never use you again and I shall make sure nobody else does!"

"Good day, Madam." The men left, casting derisive glances after them. Edgar felt angry with them and wanted to stand up for his mother, but the men departed too quickly for him to do anything but glare at their backs.

"Madam, if I could have a word." The cook, Mrs. Spence, was at the door trying to attract her attention.

"Not now, Spence. Can't you see I'm busy?"

"As you wish, Madam. Just to say I'm giving notice, Madam. And there's no meat for tonight's dinner, because Mr. Taafe won't give us any more on credit. There's fifty pounds due, Madam. Since last year, he says he has to live too, and …"

"I don't care what he says! Villain! And why are you giving notice, Mrs. Spence?"

"Because I have to live too, Madam, and you haven't paid me since January."

"You get your keep and your perks and a warm bed in a comfortable house, what more do you need? Can't you wait a little longer?"

The cook turned on her heel and left.

"They are impossible!" said Mrs. Murgatroyd. She rang the bell. "I'll get the footmen to arrange the furniture."

Lunch was a poor affair, but there was a lot of bread.

"Mother," Edgar said, taking a bite of buttered French loaf.

"Don't talk with your mouth full, Edgar."

"Mother, what will happen with the butcher if Father doesn't pay him?" he asked at an appropriate pause in chewing.

"I'm sure I don't know. His other customers pay him."

"What will Father say when he sees the new table?"

"He will fuss, but he'll get used to it."

But his father flew into a rage that evening. Edgar was sent upstairs but could hear the raised voices from his own room. The following morning, his father did not read the newspaper at breakfast and his mother did not appear. Father dismissed the footman.

"You won't be going back to school, Edgar. No, don't look so happy about it. It's bad news for you. You will not have a profession and will end up making blacklead like Charles Dickens. It's bad, I'm telling you. I am being prosecuted for my debts."

"Is this Mother's fault?"

"No, don't blame her. I promised her father I would keep her in the style to which she was accustomed, and I've broken my promises. There are a lot of things you don't understand. Bad investments and the like. It's my fault. We are going to have to leave this house before Saturday, and auction everything off."

Edgar was astounded, though he still did not fully grasp the seriousness of the situation.

"Where are we to go?"

"You and your mother will go to London."

"To Uncle Evelyn? I will be able to talk with him about the coins!"

His Father threw back his head and laughed. "My boy, Uncle Evelyn's modern coin collection will be of a greater interest to you, I hope."

"Father—will the tradesmen be paid?"

"I doubt it. We have very large debts to attend to first."

"It doesn't seem fair, Father."

"Other people pay them, Edgar. Butchers and grocers aren't going to starve, are they?"

"No, Father."

Mr. Murgatroyd got up from the table, and as he did, fell face-down upon the floor. His skin turned grey. He was motionless. The footman, hearing the thud and Edgar's cry of "Father!" sprang into the room and bent over him.

"He's dead, Master Edgar! May the Lord have mercy!"

HARD TIMES

The next few days were the worst that Edgar had ever known in his life. He could not properly grasp that he had lost his father forever, because it seemed impossible that he should have gone the way he did, suddenly. Over and over he relived the last few moments of his father's life. How could it be, that he was talking one minute, and then fell down dead the next? He missed him terribly. He had to console his mother, who was now lamenting that she was 'a poor widow without a friend in the world.'

"Uncle Evelyn will provide for us, Mother." said Edgar, sure that this old man, who he pictured to be permanently sitting up in bed with a nightcap pulled crookedly over his head, poring over a box full of sparkling gold coins, would throw open his heart and home to them.

"Hang Uncle Evelyn!" was his mother's response. "He lives forever, and my poor husband taken! If only my own poor father and mother were alive, they'd help! Everybody has run off, mark this, Edgar, for when *you* have ill-fortune, *you* will know who your friends are. I have never got on with Uncle Evelyn, he never writes to *me*, and I don't know if we'll be welcome in Knightsbridge."

The funeral was a small one. Edgar heard somebody say: "A scoundrel." And stopped speaking when he realised he was by. His heart dropped. For even Timothy kept away from him, and simply gave him a look of sympathy from a distance, when his parents were not looking. What was wrong with people? What had his father done to them, that they had turned against them all?

They returned to a house without servants. Mrs. Murgatroyd was distraught.

"You see? You see how they treat us? Just like in France at the time of the Revolution. Even Joan is gone! Joan, who I always regarded with affection, and thought she was fond of me! I do not owe her one penny, and gave her the best of my cast-offs, but she deserted me! We're in danger, Edgar, mark this. Don't sleep tonight. I am relying on you to protect me. There will be a mob of creditors with torches, led by our servants, descending upon us—take your father's pistols. Mind you don't shoot yourself."

Edgar was sure his mother exaggerated. All the same, he sat up with the pistols for a time, keeping a lookout from an upstairs window, almost wanting an excuse to fire them. But no mob came. Finally he fell asleep. When he woke, all was normal. He was greatly hungry. He'd had no dinner. He wandered to the kitchen and found some bread and cheese, and ate that.

He heard a commotion, and went around the house to see two police constables, a gentleman and several carts and labouring hands standing about.

"What do you want?" he asked abruptly.

"I have an order to seize the house and its contents," said the gentleman, who Edgar did not recognise. He pulled out a bill and showed it to him. "Open the door for us."

Edgar picked up a stick that was lying nearby, but one of the constables put out his hand and took it from him.

"Best do as he says, Master Murgatroyd. He got the Order from the magistrate. We're here to enforce it. Either we go in that way, or we'll go round; it's all the same to us."

His mother was up and dressed when he went in.

"I knew it," she said. "Did I not tell you? They will take all, and we are destitute. Oh Edgar, I shall depend upon you to restore our fortunes! Open the doors, or they will break in and murder us."

The men poured in and swarmed over the house. One of the policemen stood guard over mother and son in the kitchen to make sure they could not retrieve anything of value. It took hours.

"You have to leave now, Mrs. Murgatroyd." The bailiff, Mr. Tyler, said. "We're going to secure the property."

"Allow us to at least stay until morning, for where is a widow and child to go tonight?" she said weakly.

"Very well. I shall have my men return at nine o'clock in the morning." He was gone.

"Did they take my coins?" asked Edgar as they mounted the stairs.

"Don't be so selfish, Edgar."

"We could sell them, if they didn't."

"Oh."

As Edgar took one last look around his bare room, he noticed that one coin had rolled near the wall. Either he had been careless, or the men had forced open the box and one had fallen out somehow. He bent to retrieve it, an old Roman denarius with Caius Julius Caesar's portrait.

He was hungry again, and went to the kitchen. His mother was there.

"There is nothing to eat," she said dolefully.

"There's meat, Mother—look."

"But it's raw, Edgar."

"Build up a fire and cook it, Mother!"

"You will have to direct me, Edgar, I was never here much, but you have seen Cook do what she does, for you were always sneaking down here for tidbits."

They built up the fire for the stove, lit it, and sliced the meat. They found a frying pan and cooked it over the fire. As they were doing so, one of the servants entered. Joan had returned. Her grandmother had been a nursemaid in the Longfellow family, and had got her the place. Joan was the only servant that Mrs. Murgatroyd was fond of, because she'd loved her old Nanny.

"I'm sorry I ran away, Madam. The others said I shouldn't stay and I could not go against them. I'll stick with you, Madam and Master Edgar, no matter what happens, I will."

WHITECHAPEL

W ith Joan able to direct her mother with the right kind of firmness and deference, Edgar felt a surge of relief. They were to go to London, but Uncle Evelyn would not have notice of their coming, and he might not even be in residence. Nevertheless, they took a train to the metropolis. Joan had packed up any food that could travel, and they ate on the way. The bailiff had left some clothes and other personal possessions of little value, and those they put into boxes.

Edgar was distracted from his particular troubles by observing the big city, the intriguing, complicated criss-crossings of railway lines and sidings, the gleaming trains, majestic arches and the noise and throb of city life. Joan had been in London before and led them to Knightsbridge where they found, to their dismay, that Uncle Evelyn had gone to Switzerland for an indefinite time. The house was shut up.

They stayed in a first-class hotel for the first week. Mrs. Murgatroyd spared no expense and tried to get out of paying the bill by saying that her attorney would settle later, but the manager threatened to call the police and she was forced to hand over twenty precious pounds and seven shillings. They moved to a more modest lodging while Joan searched for accommodation. She eventually found them rooms in Whitechapel, in a courtyard near Smith's Yard. As they made their way there, through streets and alleys running with rivers of mud from recent rain, Mrs. Murgatroyd became hysterical as she sat in the hired cart among their boxes.

"The mobs! The mobs! We cannot go any farther, they will kill us!"

Joan tried to soothe her mistress, encouraging her. But people stopped to laugh and stare at this odd behaviour from a distressed lady on a cart, and a few terrorised her still further by halloing, waving and grimacing. Edgar felt a little nervous as he trudged beside them. He was glad Joan was with them. How could he ever manage his mother by himself?

They turned into a cramped courtyard filled with women hanging out their washing and young children running about barefoot. Everybody stopped and stared at the cart, the lady being handed from it, and the young gentleman.

"4 Harries Court, here we are." Joan adjusted her hat. The landlord, a man in an old grey fustian suit and a battered hat, was there with the keys. Mrs. Murgatroyd was too numbed to even notice him.

They filed in. One room. A fireplace, a coal-hole. A broken window, one rickety narrow bed, a table with one leg supported by a piece of brick, a chair and a form. A few pieces of cracked crockery and some tattered bedclothes completed their furnishings. There was no place for a servant. Edgar was going to have to sleep beside the fire, and Joan said she would live out and come daily. In truth, she had more money than her mistress, and had secured herself a room much better than this one, and was already of the opinion that she was not going to stay long. But she decided to stay at least until Edgar was bringing in some money. The boxes of gowns and other possessions filled the tiny room, giving them only a little space to live in.

"Are you going to fix that there window?" snapped Joan, at the landlord, Mr. Crabtree. "It was not broken when I took the room."

"I shall have it mended, Miss." He coughed. "As for the rent, three shillings a week—"

"We did not agree on three shillings a week!" snapped Joan. "We agreed on two shillings a week! Don't you up the rent now, or we'll leave this minute. I'm not even inclined to give you two shillings, with the broken window. And there's a new smell." She wrinkled her nose.

"If you please, they got a pig next door, and keep it in the back alley, and the smell comes in the window. It just came yesterday. Think of it as bacon."

Mrs. Murgatroyd had sunk down upon a box and pulled on Joan's skirt, hanging on to it as if for dear life.

"Joan, Joan! We can't live like this. It's worse than an attic."

"It's the only place you can afford, until Master Edgar finds work," was Joan's reply.

Edgar was hovering by the door, looking around at the crumbling buildings and general decay, as much of it as he could see through lines of billowing washing. He was on the lookout for boys his age. But Joan's words reached him, and he turned, wondering.

Mr. Crabtree left them, having obtained a week's rent in advance.

"I'll sell your gowns for you at Petticoat Lane, and what jewellery they left you will go to pawn," said Joan, trying to instil some hope. "And maybe you can take in sewing to make money."

"You will not take my gowns, nor my jewellery, and I would rather die than take in sewing!" shrieked Mrs. Murgatroyd. "You will go and look for work tomorrow, Edgar. Go to the fine offices we have seen, and tell them who you are. You have been to school, so ask for a good position, and though you are only twelve years old, you must tell them you're fifteen. And then we can move from this disgusting place. Ugh! I hear women quarrelling outside the window, the lowest of women! Their vulgar accents are nothing like I have heard before. Shut the window, Joan. The rabble!"

When Edgar woke from sleep the following morning, he found his mother sitting at the table, humming quietly to herself as if she had not a care in the world.

"Where is Lucy this morning?" she asked. "She did not come to dress me, and neither did Ellen. I do not remember giving either the day off."

"Mother, they're not here. We're not in Oxford any more. Where's Joan?"

But Joan had not come yet. Edgar stirred up the fire and boiled water and they had tea and bread. His mother's senses returned, and she again took on a disgusted and frightened look, and bade him to go out and find work.

He set off, relieved that at last he was free to wander away by himself, for his mother had forbidden him to go out alone before this. He could hardly believe the sights meeting him in the full light of day. Ragged children, begging. Saucy women in doorways who laughed at him. Men, drunk even at this early hour. Manure smells. He thought of the country and Timothy Farmer Grimsby's field and the bull. He had not had a care in the world then. Had that only been two weeks ago?

He saw Joan coming along the path toward him and ran up to her.

"Mother was quite mad this morning, asking about Lucy and all, she thought we were at home! I'm so glad you came with us."

"It's all up to you, Master Edgar," was Joan's reply. "The rent is two shillings a week, that's cheap. Food will cost more than that. And fuel for the fire. And my wages will be five shillings, I shall not require bed, but I will require some board, lunch, afternoon tea and dinner." She walked on, adjusting her hat. She was the best-dressed and the most respectable-looking female in the street.

He pondered her words for a moment. He was the man of the house now. He was twelve years old.

A BOY SEEKS WORK

He did not have to find work at just this minute, Edgar reasoned, as London was such an interesting place. He'd explore for the day and as soon as evening came, he'd go and get a situation in one of the offices he had seen yesterday in the rich part of town.

Since he'd arrived in London, he'd heard ships blasting their horns. He reckoned he'd go and see them. So he turned his direction to the docklands. The streets turned into alleys; people and shops were numerous—sail makers, marine outfitters, food stalls, pawnbrokers. Gulls swooped upon the streets to peck at crumbs and offal. He stopped to stare at a bearded man in fine uniform, brass buttons shining, the captain of a ship, perhaps! Then his attention was captured by a dark man in a brightly-patterned shirt and a straw hat bedecked with ribbons, carrying a parrot in a cage. Adventure was here!

He became aware that three boys were watching him on the corner, and as he approached he stuck his hands in his pockets, tried to look as if he didn't care, and whistled a tune.

"Who're you, then?" said one of the boys who stood in front of him, blocking his path.

"Who're *you?*" asked Edgar. The boys were about his own age, dressed in rags, but one had a peaked tartan cap and another had a dirty, but fancy cravat a great deal too large for his thin neck. The third was a small, but tough boy with a pock-marked face.

"We 'avent seen you 'ere afore. Does your mother know you're out?" said with great derision.

"I 'avent seen you afore either," replied Edgar, mimicking his speech.

"I been 'ere orright, you're the stranger."

"So, this is England, isn't it? England's a free country, isn't it?"

"*Isn't it?*" they mocked him. One pulled at his jacket, another pulled off his cap.

This was too much. Edgar sprang to retrieve his cap and his pride, but found himself splayed upon the footpath, kicked by several pairs of bare feet. They were not hard kicks, they were merely meant to show him who was boss. But someone was untying his boots. He scrambled up somehow, and ran, his shirt hanging out, but he had, as he had gone, snatched the tartan cap from one of his tormentors, and this he stuck on his head as he sprinted away. When he stopped running and looked back, there was no sign of them. Then he realised he was almost on the Thames, so he forgot about them.

He slipped inside a set of large gates when it opened for a cart, and he was on the quays. Everybody was having a jolly time. Deafening clangs and hammerings met his ears. Foremen shouted. A line of sooty men in overalls hauled bags of coal from a barge like a line of ants coming down the gangway. They deposited the coal in a warehouse and filed back for more. They looked tough. Edgar wondered if his mother would mind if he got a job as a coal-hauler. Walking along, he saw a group of dark sailors disembarking a ship, with jaunty hats and wide trousers, their kits slung over their shoulders. They chattered in a strange language.

Then a loud noise got his attention, at the next berth a large crane had just deposited a load onto the deck of a ship and clanged thunderously when the chains were loosened.

"Is that a steam crane?" he asked the man directing operations, the coal forgotten. "I'm looking for work. Can I get a job operating that?"

"It's steam, lad, brand-new. We have no vacancy, and there's a queue of men wanting to train at it. How did you get in here? Now off you go."

He left, quite disappointed, until his attention was caught by a boy climbing high onto the rigging of another ship with the agility of a squirrel. This he watched with amazement, until he felt his stomach grumbling. It was time to eat luncheon, and he remembered that he had passed several food stalls, so he left the docks again, avoiding the street where the boys were. He bought a pork-pie, thinking that it was the shape of Joan's hat, and wondering if he'd tell her, but decided not to. He wiped his hands on his jacket, adjusted the cap, and set off for more sightseeing. This time, he thought he'd go to a railway station.

There, he saw a boy begging. He had a penny, so he gave it to him. He then wondered what it was like to beg, and decided, since nobody knew him and that his mother would never get to hear of it, to try it out for a lark. He decided to be an orphan, and held out his hand, "Poor orphan, no mother, no father," he said mournfully. But though people glanced his way, no help was forthcoming.

"If you want money, why don't you sell your boots?" said a young man, mocking him.

So that was why it wasn't working! He didn't look poor! He quickly took off his boots and socks and hid them behind a seat. He begged for an hour, and collected quite a number of pennies, halfpennies, and one very old lady told him he was a very unfortunate boy indeed and gave him sixpence. After he got tired of that, and a policeman was glaring at him, he decided that he'd had enough. He went to retrieve his boots but they were not there. A short time later he passed an urchin girl who was carrying boots that looked very like his, and he was sure of it when she gave him a smug smile as she tightened them to her chest, but he could not fight a girl, so he passed on.

It was time to look for a situation. After purchasing a cream bun from a baker's shop, and wiping his hands down his shirt, he followed a coach and four to an area that had large buildings and where he was sure there were offices. But all the doormen seemed to have a common goal in keeping him from entering their premises, and where there was no doorman, somebody from an office within took great umbrage at his presence, so he made off, and found his way back to Whitechapel. He was hungry again, and he hoped that Joan would have a good meal ready. He did not miss his boots, but worried that his mother would notice they were gone, and mothers could be particular about things like that.

"Who are you?" cried his mother in alarm, when he came in. "Why are you here? Leave immediately!"

"I declare, Madam, it's Master Edgar under all that dirt! He looks like he's been pulled though an 'edge backwards. Where are your boots, Master Edgar?"

"I gave them to a poor orphan girl."

"Look at the dreadful state you are in!" cried Mrs. Murgatroyd. "What happened?"

"And where's your cap?" demanded Joan, who was acting almost like a mother too.

"I swapped it for this."

"A bad bargain!" Joan sneered.

"But did you get a situation?" cried Mrs. Murgatroyd.

"Of course, I did, Mother. And they paid me, too." He said proudly, emptying his pockets of a collection of copper coins and one bright sixpence.

"Good boy. But what an odd way to pay you. Where did you work?"

"Down by the railway station. I got a good place."

"I'm so proud of you, dear boy! Let me count it."

But Joan was staring at him with great scepticism. Why were adults so difficult to please?

"Twelve farthings, twenty-two halfpennies, sixteen pennies, and one sixpence. Three shillings in total! Oh, darling boy, you'll make eighteen shillings a week! It's hardly enough, but it will do for a start!"

24

THE SWELL

Cleaned up again, and wearing his spare shoes, Edgar set off the following morning. He did not know what to do today, but thought something would occur to him as he walked along, kicking an old tin can before him. No school! What a paradise! He could do what he liked all day long and nobody bossed him around, no parent, no teacher. He stopped to throw a stick for a dog, and the dog followed him, heedless of his repeated orders to '*go home.*'

He'd go and see the ships again. The scene was the same as yesterday, except there was a new coal barge in. Nobody took any notice of him.

He was supposed to come home with money, but he didn't quite know how to earn it today. Begging was all very well, but he didn't want to lose this pair of shoes. He left the quays and keeping near the water, walked for a bit. The streets grew seedier. He was now in a place filled with houses of entertainment with garish signs and rude posters. Girls in bawdy dress swaggered along and some halloed to him. On the wharf, children waded in the dirty water with baskets on their hips. They picked up lumps of coal and pieces of wood. The smells were putrid, a mixture of fish and all kinds of dirt and filth.

Turning toward the arches of a place called the Adelphi, he became aware that there were many people around, boys like the ones he'd seen yesterday, and older boys, some poorly dressed, and a few better-dressed swells. He became watchful in case he encountered any like those he had met the day before. He had an uneasy feeling. London was good fun yesterday, but today it had a sinister air. The boys were staring at him so he stared back as he walked along. He knew he should look as if he was on familiar ground. The dog was still following him.

"You're new." The statement came from a swell some years older than he. He was dressed in a top hat and a good suit with a showy cravat. He even had a pair of white gloves, or they would be white if they got a good wash. His front teeth were missing, and he carried a cane.

"Is that against the law or something?" Edgar asked. A group of younger boys had gathered around him.

"Oh, the law. Are you a copper's boy?"

"No, my father's dead."

The man produced a small bottle from his inside pocket, and unscrewed the cap. "'Ospitality," he said. "We're a welcoming set of people around 'ere."

"What is it?"

"Gin."

"No thanks."

"Why not? You afeard of a little drop?"

Edgar said the first thing that came into his head.

"Gin makes me come out in spots." This last word was repeated with merriment by the boys around him.

"Got anyfink in your pockets? Any brass?" asked a grubby boy of around fourteen, tugging at the hem of his jacket.

"Noffink," said Edgar, taking on the patois. "I got no money, if that's what you want. I had some yesterday, but I gave it all to my mother."

"That's the right thing to do," said the swell, who the others were calling Looking-Glass Jack. "Yeah, I agree with that an' all. It's a good thing to do, support your widowed mother. Do you want to earn money today?"

Edgar felt that his luck was in after all. Glass Jack invited him to enter one of the archways. Another world lurked there. This was a wide arch, and it was dark except for a lamp or candle lit wherever a group of boys gathered. It seemed to be their lodging, for there were mats and mattresses and coats strewn about, and some very young boys were sleeping on them. There were dirty cups and plates on the ground. As Glass Jack led the way with a rushlight, Edgar saw a large rat upon a plate, gnawing a scrap of meat. He felt chilled. He did not like this place, and resolved to get away as soon as he could, after he had earned money.

"How much do I get?" he asked Glass Jack.

"Sixpence."

"That's not enough. I have to bring home three shillings."

"You can stay with us all day, we'll get you your three shillings, but you 'ave to do as I say."

"Agreed, then." He set out with them, the dog following.

"Now see 'ere, this is what you 'ave to do. There's a group of us going out soon, up to Bedford Square. We're going to do a job. You, you're going to pretend you don't know us, and you 'ave to distract a certain gentleman with questions about something, ask him directions, the way to Westminster for instance."

"What kind of job are you going to do?" asked Edgar.

"We're going to steal a few flowers to sell, see?" said Glass Jack.

"All right." Edgar was mystified as to why they couldn't wait until he was out of sight to pick the flowers, but he did not question. They set out. En route, he saw several of the boys steal apples from fruit stalls. He thought of the time he'd robbed Farmer Hayes' orchard, and this was no different, so when he got the chance he took one too. He was hungry.

The boys set a watch in a park lined with bushes, from where they had a good view of the row of fine houses. Edgar did not see any gardens but he supposed them to be in the backs.

"Watch number twenty. He always comes out when the clock strikes one," said Glass Jack. "Just afore that, I want you to walk up the street. And look lost, like. Then stop 'im and ask the way to Westminster. Tuck in your shirt, look respectable. Your cap is rotten. Jimmy, lend 'im your cap."

Jimmy reluctantly handed over his cap and at the appointed time Edgar walked up the street. The gentleman came out of the house and he stopped him to ask the way to Westminster. While the man was engaged in giving directions, he was rushed by several of the boys, who pinned him against a railing and divested him of a silver watch, a silk handkerchief and a wallet, delivering a few strong punches when he tried to fight back. Edgar stood rooted to the spot, a look of horror on his face. He turned and ran away, away from the boys. This was criminal. This was wrong. He ran until he was sure they could not catch up with him. He had no sixpence; he wanted no part of stealing. Taking flowers was one thing—flowers grew again. Attacking a man to rob him was quite another.

He had no option but to beg for a few hours in different locations. Today, it was not a game. He hid his shoes carefully this time. Mid-afternoon, a train discharged a class of schoolboys and their masters. The boys were chattering and laughing. Suddenly, he wished he was one of them. They took no notice of him and one of the masters looked upon him with disdain.

He returned home with less money than the day before, and felt dejected. London was not so great after all.

The gravity of his situation, and that of his mother, hit him. They were poor, and if he did not get money for both of them, they would starve or have to live under an arch and he would have to steal and protect his food from rats.

The dog had followed him all day long. At least he had one friend, and he took the scraps of mutton stew and fed him' with it. His mother would not let him inside, and Joan disapproved heartily; the dog would have to find himself a little place to sleep somewhere. He pondered what to call him and decided on 'Caesar.'

25

A NEW FRIEND

Caesar went everywhere with Edgar. One day, when they were crossing the High Street, he heard a female voice call, "Mitch! Mitch!" Caesar bolted in the direction of the voice and jumped into the arms of a woman who was younger than Edgar's mother, and yet not young. She wore a gown with an ornate shawl, and a bonnet with frills. She looked a little like one of the women he saw in doorways beckoning to men, but not as garish, but he approached warily. She seemed to love Mitch, and Mitch certainly loved her, so she must be all right.

"Oh, Mitch, I thought you were dead." The dog licked the woman's face all over.

"Is he yours?" he asked, with disappointment.

"Yes, but—I fear he ran away."

"Ran away? Why?"

The woman put the dog down, and he trotted back to Edgar's side.

"He belongs to you now, doesn't he?" She smiled. Her eyes were gentle.

"Yes, I call him Caesar."

"A good name, Caesar. Do you live around here then, Master—em?"

"I'm Edgar Murgatroyd. My mother and I live at Harries Court, we moved here some time ago from Oxford."

"I'm Caroline Davey, and I came from Devonshire, from a little village named Fernleigh. I've been here fifteen years, I'm a milliner by trade. Edgar, you speak well, don't you?"

Edgar was surprised, but then he had noticed that she too spoke well, even a little like his mother.

"We used to be rich, but my father died. My mother and I had to move here."

"I'm going in the direction of Ellen Street, shall we walk along together? I too have had a misfortune, and I like to talk to people who have suffered the same circumstances. I did not choose to come here, as you did not."

Edgar told her about the bankruptcy, and his mother's dependence upon him, and she was very intrigued and sorry to hear his story. And she told him hers, as much as was proper, that she and her brother had been cheated out of an inheritance, and had come to London to stay with a cousin. One day, she became quite lost, and a very bad thing happened to her, causing her to be unable to leave the district ever again.

"I say, that's too bad," Edgar said, not understanding. "What about your brother?"

"I do not know where he is now."

"But who do you live with?"

"Friends. This is as far as I'm going, Edgar. And if you want Mitch—or Caesar, keep him. One of the people in the house doesn't like him, and ill-treated him, and no doubt that is why he ran away."

Edgar was sorry to part with her. She felt like a friend already. "Miss Davey—will you visit my mother?" He asked in an inspiration. "I know she'd like you."

Miss Davey hesitated as she smiled quietly to herself.

"I'm sure I would be happy to, but tell her first, that you have met me, and give her my history as I have given it to you."

"Oh, I will, Miss Davey. Thank you!" With Caesar by his side, he set off again.

TURN FOR THE WORSE

Edgar decided that day that he would try the docks for a job. But there was a line of men before him, day labourers who had not succeeded at the first call of the day and were hoping for another chance. He was forced to beg again, which had become very tiresome to him. People were beastly. Schoolboys made fun of him, but that afternoon, reminded of his better days as related to Miss Davey, he threw a string of Latin at one of them, which astonished them all. He saw one of the masters look at him with great curiosity. He shook his tin can and resumed his chant: *"Orphan! Halfpenny for an 'ungry orphan!"* It sounded so hollow, and he was not an orphan, but he felt like one, and he was hungry, was becoming thinner, and his clothes had not been washed in many days.

Then he saw, alighting the train behind the schoolboys, the very man who had been robbed in Bedford Square. He looked down. He wondered if he should scarper to another location. After the next train, then. But only ten minutes later, he found his shoulder grasped roughly from behind, and twisting about in protest, he found a police constable staring down at him.

He hoped it was about begging. He knew it was illegal, on account of some friendly beggars he had met, who had told him he should have matches on him, or peppermint lozenges, for when the police were about. Selling was legal, begging was not. But the constable had more upon his mind than to investigate how he was making a living. He marched him to the station, where he was pushed into a cell. There, the Bedford Square man was called, and he looked in through the bars at him and said,

"Yes, that's the boy who stopped me to ask for directions. He is of the gang."

"I didn't know what they were going to do!" he protested. "I didn't know they were going to attack you! Honest!"

Edgar told the police the truth, including 'Glass Jack' who had been behind the entire crime, and described the other fellows. He owed them no loyalty!

The next several days were very hard, except that he was fed regularly. He was on remand, and his mother came to see him. The first thing she said to him was that Joan was gone—when the money ran out, she left. Mrs. Murgatroyd was very bitter about this. A true servant would go through hunger and peril for her mistress!

"No doubt they are feeding you well in here, but I am existing on offal. I am going to have to lower myself in a way I have never had to do before, or I will die. I must have a protector!"

"Are you feeding Caesar?" Edgar wished to know.

"All you care about is your dog. I do not know where he is. Good riddance."

He was visited by Miss Davey, who put his mind at rest about his dog. She had taken him back for now or for as long as necessary. "Now to more important matters, Edgar. You need counsel. And I'll provide it. Don't worry about the money."

When court sat, his counsel argued for him strongly, his youth, his misfortune, his innocence, and he was given only one month's detention. He discovered that Glass Jack was no stranger to the court, and the Judge was severe on him. Despite pleas from his counsel, he was given five years penal servitude, and the other boys three years each. Glass Jack did not look so dapper in the dock.

Court was a deep shock to him, as was jail, which was solitary confinement with an hour of exercise with the other prisoners once a day. He had plenty of time to think and he began to pray as his nanny had taught him when he was younger. Dear old Nanny White! He felt closer to her than to his mother! What would she say if she saw him now? Nanny used to say: *'Always do the right thing, the kind thing.'* He was determined to be very wise in the future, and honest, and never get into trouble again. He'd do the meanest manual labour rather than fall in with a gang of thieves.

The morning after his release, he went to the docks seeking work, joining the throngs of desperate men who surged toward the ganger in charge of hiring the labour. He was unsuccessful every morning and spent the rest of the day seeking work outside the docks. Eventually he was taken on at a tanning yard deep in Bermondsey. It was obnoxious, stinking labour. His pay was very meagre, but now he only had himself and his dog to keep. His mother had disappeared from Whitechapel, saying she was going to try her fortune in the Haymarket, as a paid hostess in a Gentleman's Club, where she was expected to spend the evenings dancing with the clients. She had great confidence in her charms and hoped to marry one of the gentlemen.

Edgar lived in a lodging house of the lowest kind near the tannery. But whenever he could, he went to the area of the docklands known as Gullseye. He had got to know some of the coalmen working there. After six months, he had a visit one Sunday from Denny, one of the coal-haulers, to tell him that a man had fallen and broken his leg and was not likely to work again for a long time. Edgar went to the docklands very early the next morning, Denny advocated for him and he was taken on. It was a piece of great good luck. The work was relentless and back-breaking, but infinitely better than degreasing wet, fresh cowhide.

27

BIRD OF PARADISE

Aidah Murgatroyd invented an interesting past for herself. Attired in elegant gowns from her other life, with her hair done in soft ringlets, and capped with soft satin and dove's feathers, she told her dancing partners that she was Maria Hernandez, the widow of a South American merchant, and that upon his death she had returned to England, only to find that her family had emigrated to America. As many of her dancing partners had assumed names also, nobody asked her to elaborate. Occasionally, she was asked if she had any children, to which she replied that she had not. After all, she had told the owners that she was twenty-four, eight years younger than she really was. With skilful application of powder and creams, she knew she could pass for a younger woman.

She soon gave up the idea that one of the gentlemen would want to marry her. They were low men, perhaps not in rank, but in their morals. Unhappily, she decided that if she wanted one of these men to provide her with a better life, she had to give something in return. A year passed, and another, before she achieved the next best situation to marriage.

One of her regular dance partners was a man about fifty years of age, and after a year he proposed to settle her in a nice flat in the West End with a lady's maid, a cook, a parlourmaid and a phaeton. She was happy to have this good life, and held her head up when she drove her little conveyance around, and one day when Edgar was hauling coal he was surprised to see his mother standing on the dockside, dressed elegantly in pale blue, with an elaborate hat and a fur muff. He dropped off the coal and went to her. She held up a white kid-gloved hand.

"Edgar, what a dreadful figure you make, covered in coal dust, do not come any nearer to me, please."

"What do you want, Mother? Have you left that old bounder yet?"

"How dare you, Edgar! Fourteen years old and you speak like that to your mother!"

"Mother, I told you I was earning regular money now. You can come back to live with me. I'm doing honest work, I'll support you."

"No, Edgar. I'm too used to this life. I cannot stand being poor. And before you judge me, you know that Miss Davey, who you seem to have adopted as some sort of aunt, is worse than me. A great deal worse, for I have confined myself to one special man, whereas she will favour anybody who will throw her sixpence."

This robbed him of speech, and he watched her walk away from him, being careful to avoid a grimy patch of ground, and he followed her briefly until she alighted her phaeton and set off smartly.

"Murgatroyd, are you working today or not?" snarled the ganger in his ear. "Who was that fancy piece?"

Two minutes later he was dismissed for knocking the ganger to the ground. He walked away with determination. He was troubled that his mother was the mistress of a dishonourable man, and that Miss Davey, who he liked very much and looked up to like an older sister, was a prostitute. He was bitterly disappointed in both of them.

Edgar was becoming good at keeping his ears open and his eyes peeled. He had heard of a new warehouse in Lanyard Lane looking for hands. He made his way there and secured a job. Older now, and taller, and tougher, he cut a good figure to a prospective employer. His dark eyes were direct and honest and held a determination that impressed people. He had developed strong muscles and was able to work hard and rarely went sick.

28

A HAPPY HOME

Edgar moved to a working man's lodging house, a decent place. Most of the men were engaged in trade around the docklands area, either as labourers, sailmakers, cobblers or ironworkers. He was a popular lad and his friends were numerous. In their free time, if they did not go out, they stayed at home playing cards. Some of the men could not read or write, and as it became known that Edgar had these skills, and could write well without labouring over it or misspelling, some of the men asked him to write letters for them. He always obliged cheerfully. The men sometimes paid him, which he hardly wanted to take, but sometimes it was a matter of pride on their part, and he always accepted when they said they 'could never ask him again, if they couldn't pay.' He was glad to earn a little extra, small as it was. He always carried the Roman coin with him. It was a tangible reminder of when times were better with him. Sometimes he wondered how much it was worth.

Edgar was careful of his money. It was hard-won and easily lost. He remembered how his mother used to urge him to learn how to play cards; she had never envisaged poker games in a rough lodging in London's East End. The stakes were never high; if a man wanted to play serious poker, or had the desire to gamble more than was good for him, he went elsewhere.

Some of the men, like him, had done time in a jail and never wanted to go back. They all knew boys and men who had fallen in with a bad crowd and ended up going repeatedly to prison, they were acquainted with scoundrels and cheats and heard gossip of slick burglars and picklocks, but to the men in 32 Kendall Street, this kind of living was alien to them.

"It's all luck, if you ask me," said Kevin Black to him one evening. "You were lucky not to have been in for long, and when you came out, you got a job. Some can't, they get hungry and go back to where they know there's food to be got. Like those pitiful boys under the Adelphi arches."

"Some of them were little more than infants. I wonder what's become of them. I do wish I had a trade though," Edgar added regretfully. "But it costs money to be apprenticed. I'd like to be a baker or a cook, something like that."

"Whenever you cook here, everybody stays in for supper."

Edgar got into morose moods sometimes. Alone in the world, he rarely saw his mother. She was a bird of paradise, and he never went to her apartment. He was sure it would disgust him to see her in her gilded cage. Her words about Miss Davey had caused him to give *her* a wide berth. He could hardly believe it of her. He wondered where his own life would lead, whether he would ever get a chance for more education, whether he was doomed to labouring all of his life, and more than that, whether he would ever be part of a real family again. He suffered a great loneliness of heart.

He went for long walks on Sundays, often on his own, liking to be solitary after a week of company at work and at his lodgings. One Sunday, as he turned the corner of Kendall Street, he came by a woman a little older than he, who was sitting on a low wall, holding her ankle in a painful way and groaning.

"What's the matter, Miss?"

"I tripped over that—" she pointed to a loose stone on the pathway "—and fear I can't walk back to my 'ouse. If you would you be so good as to lend me your arm, I might manage it, if you are not in any 'urry and it isn't out of your way. It's not far."

He offered his arm and she took it. She limped along for a time, and they began to talk. Her name was Miss Donnelly. She lived in Hamm Street, only a quarter of an hour away. Miss Donnelly was charming and very grateful to her assistant and implored him to come in and show himself to her parents, that they would be reassured that the boy who had brought her home was *a good respectable young gentleman.* Edgar was happy with the description; did he not aspire to all of that? He was brought in, great thanks was rendered, he was made to sit down and drink tea and he took his leave with the feeling that he had met very good, nice people; when her father, Mr. Donnelly, asked him to come back and visit them, he was very glad to say he would.

When he related the incident when he got home, a bricklayer named Dorry was a little sceptical.

"Be careful, Murgy. You're still a young lad. Don't you go falling for Miss Donnelly or doing anything stupid, like."

But Edgar did not listen. He thought that Dorry was over-reacting. He was aged about forty, and very cautious, was Dorry.

He returned to the Donnelly house and was received warmly. They were such nice people, and encouraged him to talk of himself, and he found himself giving a history of his family. Of course, he did not mention his mother and her disgrace—these good people would end the acquaintance immediately.

"Oh, you must be a fair writer, if you went to school for so long," said Mrs. Donnelly, the picture of domestic tranquillity, her hair in a lacy mob cap, a light shawl about her shoulders as she knitted socks for Mr. Donnelly.

"I am not too bad, I suppose. I was taught well, by a good Master."

"I do so wish I could write better," sighed Miss Donnelly, whose first name as Eliza. She was seated on a low stool beside her father. "If I did, Papa, I would write to Mr. 'Awkins, I would."

"Forget about it, child," said her father, the very picture of paternal affection, patted his daughter's fair head. "We'll let it be, and manage some'ow."

But to Edgar's dismay, Miss Donnelly began to weep.

"Write? If you need a letter written, I can oblige you," he said. "It would be no trouble."

"It would be too much trouble," said her father, puffing his pipe. "It is also a delicate matter."

"A very delicate matter," said Mrs. Donnelly. "A promise broken."

"Oh Mama, do not speak of it!" cried poor Eliza.

"Now that we have spoken at all, I think we owe Edgar the favour of enlightening 'im," said Mr. Donnelly.

"Oh really, I'd rather not—" said Edgar hastily, lest they felt they had to.

"Of course, you'd rather not. We would lose your good opinion immediately," sighed Mrs. Donnelly, laying down her needles with a sad and dejected air.

"I am sure I would never think badly of you," cried Edgar.

"Well then, what is the 'arm?" said the father. "My dear Eliza, if you cannot bear to hear the history, you may go upstairs."

"I will bear it, Papa," said the girl, bravely.

"It is like this," began Mr. Donnelly. "Last summer, our daughter Eliza, who you see 'ere, was courted by a young man named Mr. Hawkins, a Mr. Peter Hawkins. He seemed in every way to be a good, upright young man with a profession—a barrister-at-law."

"He was above us, and we should have been more alert," said Mrs. Donnelly.

Eliza's head was down; she twisted her hands in her lap.

"Mr. Hawkins was very attentive, told our daughter he loved 'er, and marriage was mentioned, all that, and next thing, she was with child. But before she knew, Mr. Hawkins had vanished."

"Oh Papa, did you have to say so, about the child!" she burst out.

"Eliza, it's the truth. We don't blame you. You were sixteen. He was twenty-eight. So, Edgar, only three weeks ago, I went to visit Mr. Hawkins, only to find out I could not get past the snooty butler. I was turned away, Edgar."

"But that was dreadful!" Edgar said with anger.

"And that wasn't all. Only last week, I saw his engagement announced in the newspaper. What do you think of that?"

"He sounds like a villain, a cad."

"So I have thought of writin' a letter, except that my writin' is not good."

"Nor mine," said Mrs. Donnelly.

"I could not, he would know my hand, and throw away the letter without opening it," sniffed Eliza.

"And you cannot write well in any case," her mother reminded her.

"Oh, that too!"

"If you would like me to pen a letter for you, I would be happy to do it, all you need to do is dictate it to me." Edgar offered.

"Oh, we could not ask—"

"Actually, it is not to Mr. 'Awkins we should write," Mrs. Donnelly said. "But to his fiancée, to warn her of 'im. Scoundrel!"

"Oh no, Charlotte, to 'im first." Mr. Donnelly seemed to have it all thought out. "We have pen and paper 'ere—would you be able to do it now?"

"Certainly," said Edgar. He drew himself nearer to the table.

'Dear Sir, it is with a heavy heart I write to you, but I was turned away last week. I, the father of Miss Elizabeth Donnelly, who you seduced and left in distress, am compelled to appeal to you to do the right thing by her. We do not expect marriage, the differences in our rank, and the fact that you are now an engaged man, makes that impossible. My wife and I request the sum of two hundred pounds for my daughter and your child that she carries. The bearer of this letter will await a reply.'

"You are not going to post it, then, Richard?" asked Mrs. Donnelly.

"No, I will ask somebody, a friend, to deliver it and await a response. It is the best way, otherwise it will get thrown into the fire."

"But who, Papa?" cried Eliza.

"I do not know, I will think of somebody—a trustworthy person."

"Where does he live?" asked Edgar.

"At Parkway Avenue, in Westminster."

"But that is not far. I can oblige you," Edgar said.

Their gratitude was very touching. Eliza got up and made him tea and it was served with warm apple tart and cream.

He brought the letter back to the lodging house from where he would deliver it the following day, which was Monday. He told Kevin about it.

"If I was you, I wouldn't 'ave got involved," Kevin said, frowning. "You 'ardly know these people."

But Edgar was undeterred.

PARKWAY AVENUE

Edgar waited in vain for a response to the letter at Parkway. The butler told him that Mr. Hawkins would fetch the police if he did not make himself scarce right away. He went to the Donnellys and related his tale, feeling that he had failed.

They told him not to worry, and made him tea and put slices of chocolate cake before him. Mrs. Donnelly fussed over him like a mother hen, how he wished his own mother was like her! And Mr. Donnelly was a loving father and a good, hardworking husband—the signs of his dedication to family were everywhere, a comfortable home with a roaring fire, a dresser filled with all the things a home needed, food in the larder and the kettle always on the boil. Edgar wanted, more than anything, to feel part of a family. Eliza was sweet, poor girl! He had tender feelings for the poor innocent who was seduced by a man who had taken advantage of her.

"What will you do now?" he asked them.

"I want to tell his fiancée what a rotter he is," said Mrs. Donnelly.

"Miss Brierly is not our business," said her husband. "Our daughter is our business. But I think we will have to write a stronger letter, in which we will threaten to *tell* Miss Brierly, if he does not provide for our poor Eliza."

There was an expectant silence, and Edgar at last said: "I will write it, if you wish."

"Are you sure, dear boy?" asked Mrs. Donnelly, cutting him another slice of cake while her husband threw some more coal on the fire.

"I am sure," he said.

And so it was written, a stronger letter, threatening to inform Miss Brierly if he did not provide money for Miss Donnelly, who had been so cruelly used.

"Would you be so obliging as to deliver it again?" asked Mrs. Donnelly.

Edgar hesitated. The first letter was all very well, but delivering the second, which contained a threat, he balked at. But several pairs of eyes were looking at him with hope. The fire crackled and Mr. Donnelly drew slowly on his pipe, his eyes never leaving Edgar.

"It is too much to ask, I fear," Mrs. Donnelly sighed, "Although you need not wait, really you need not. He can respond in his own time, I am sure he will." She sighed again, a long sigh that seemed to hold all the trouble in the world in it.

There was a despondent silence.

"I will wait for his response," said Edgar at last.

After work the following day, he cleaned himself up and took the letter to Parkway Avenue. The butler took it and stared hard at it and then at him, before leaving him on the doorstep to take it upstairs.

"Come in please," he said upon reappearing. Edgar followed him in and waited in a plush drawing room. It was so like the one of his childhood that it made him feel nostalgic. There were photographs on the walls, groups of people, a family. They had sons, two—no three. And a daughter, a pretty girl. Families were everywhere, rich, poor—but he had none, and while he did not want to feel sorry for himself, he felt it greatly that he was just a lodger in a lodging house, with no home.

The door was wrenched open and two angry gentlemen in smoking jackets came in and slammed it behind them. One was young, and the other older —a father and son. Edgar rose from his chair.

"What is this?" the younger man shouted, thumping the letter he held with a closed fist. "Extortion, isn't it? I don't even know this girl, if she exists!"

"You do know her, she's a Miss Eliza Donnelly—"

"Rubbish! And you think we're going to shell out two hundred pounds to you? Who are you working for? Who?" The older man was furious.

"I'm a labourer at Messrs. Benson and Carroll, they make—"

"It doesn't matter. We know your game." They sat down and motioned to him to sit also. They were by the door, and he by the fireplace. They said nothing, just looked at him with cold, calm hostility. They were like jailers, and he became uneasy—why would they not want his departure? What were they waiting for? He thought he'd have another try.

"But are you going to assist Miss Donnelly? You left her in a state of distress, and her mother and father, very good people, are very cut up about the whole affair. They don't expect marriage—they need help to look after her, and the baby—"

They did not reply, they did not even deign to glance at him.

"If your answer is no, then I will be upon my way—" he rose, now becoming anxious.

"You are not going anywhere, you young vagabond." stated the older man. "How old are you? Sixteen?"

There was a kerfuffle in the hall, and the door was wrenched open again. This time, two police constables burst in, with the butler close behind them.

"There's the fraudster, Constables. Arrest him," the old man said.

Edgar could not believe that this was happening.

"I haven't committed any crime!" he shouted. "You keep away from me!" He tried to make an escape though them, but it was useless. He was secured and marched off and into the waiting police van.

He told his story at the police station, giving them the address of the Donnelly family. A constable was dispatched. Edgar was shoved into a remand cell.

There was another prisoner there, stretched out on a bunk.

It was very late when the constable returned.

"No such people," he said. "A family named Cotter took it about six weeks ago, but there is no trace of them there now. They were seen to leave this evening in a hackney, with baggage."

The other prisoner snorted.

"You haven't got the address right." Edgar countered. "11 Hamm Street." But the address was the correct one.

Edgar sank back upon his bunk with a feeling of dread in his heart. What had happened? Where were the Donnellys?

"Tell me about it, boy," said the other prisoner, an older man with scarred face and rough hands. Two of his fingers were missing. His name was Wally. "Time passes slowly in here. It had better be a good story, and then I'll explain it to you, cos I'm sure I can."

Edgar told him all, from beginning to end.

"Someone where you live recommended you as a scriver, an' these people set it all up," Wally said.

"Sounds like Moll Driver and that other fellow, no relation to 'er, but they works together. She'll never finish that sock. It's part of the act. I dunno who this Eliza is. It's a well-known trick. They look for the Engagements in the papers, then they spin a yarn, and write to the man, threatening to tell the fiancée that the man she's marrying 'as a bad past, and demanding money to keep their mouths shut. Most men just pay up to make them go away. Can't stand the doubt over their character, see? And anyways, many of 'em have a past, and get nervous. Two hundred pounds was a bit much though. Fifty he might 'ave given to get rid of them. They got greedy."

Edgar still did not understand why he had to have a role in this. Why could they not have written the letter themselves?

"First, maybe the coppers knows their writing, and second, you were the dupe. One followed you there, in a cab most likely, and when they saw the coppers going to the 'ouse, off they goes and packs up and leaves. They're so used to moving off quickly it don't take 'em longer than five minutes. So the question now is, will the jury believe you were a dupe?"

The jury did not. Edgar was sentenced to two years hard labour. He had plenty of time to think and wonder who in his lodging house had told of his ability to write. He went over every man, every character, but could not pin it on anybody. But somebody had set him up.

Kevin and Sorry were his first visitors. Edgar felt wretched. His fingers were sore and pitted already from ten hours of picking oakum day after day in his cell. Oakum was old rope, tarred, and the prisoners had to spend their time unplaiting the strands. It was rough work and extremely boring. Time dragged. He spent his hours hating the Donnellys/Cotters, whatever their names were. All the more so because they had seemed like a good, nice family and it was all false. At least Dorry did not say 'I told you so.'

One day, the warden threw open his door. "Your sister's here," he said.

"I don't—" then he recollected himself. Was it his mother?

But the figure in the bonnet and cloak was Miss Davey. She smiled wanly at him, a sympathetic, fond smile.

"What happened?" she asked him. He related the story. "I bet you don't believe me, though," he said bitterly.

"You are mistaken. I believe you. There are evil people in the world." She looked down. "After I came here, I met some of them." She said no more, but produced a bag of currant buns, and looked at the warden, who nodded his consent.

"Does your mother know, Edgar?"

"Yes, she came to court one day, and left without speaking to me. Then she visited me here after I was sentenced." The memory angered him, for she was not interested in hearing what had happened to him and assumed his guilt. She had spent the visit weeping into her silk handkerchief and saying that she was a terrible mother, and that it was too late now for her to take him in hand—his character was set. He gave up trying to make her see that he was innocent, and ended up trying to console *her*.

"Your counsel is trying to find the Cotters, or whatever their names are."

"Tell him not to bother. I can't afford counsel anyway. But if I ever see those people again, I could —" he snarled.

"Edgar, if I might give you a little advice—try not to spend your days hating and resenting. Oh I know it's hard. Believe me, I have suffered this!"

"Have you been in prison?" he looked up in surprise.

"No," she said softly, avoiding his eyes. "Not a walled prison like this. But I have been in prison in my mind—hating, hating and hating. It doesn't do. It can eat you and ruin your life—no, Edgar, your life is not ruined, you got two years, not twenty. You'll still be young after you come out."

He pondered this for the rest of the day. It was all very well for Miss Davey to tell him not to hate, but the feeling was there.

Pray, said the still, small voice. *Pray. Ask for a Bible and pray.*

ESTELLA COURT

One and a half years later, Edgar was released early. Kevin and Dorry found him a job in the foundry where Dorry's brother was foreman. His brother had taken some persuading and was sceptical but was prepared to give him a chance. Edgar was very grateful. His innocence in the affair was widely believed. He felt stupid, though. How could he not have seen that he was being used?

Prison had altered him forever. He was a man of eighteen now, and a very cautious man. He'd never do anybody a good turn again.

He was allowed to move back into the lodging, and he had a joyous reunion with Caesar, who remembered him. He was lucky, for the lodging house did not welcome convicts, but his story was known. He'd concluded that he would never know if he had been set-up initially by someone there, or that it was said innocently to the Cotters that there was a lad who wrote well, a good obliging sort. All they had to do then was for Eliza to await his coming out of the house, and run to the corner where she pretended to have sprained her ankle.

In his last year, he had been allowed to mingle with the other prisoners, a blessing and a curse. For there, he had come into contact with many criminal characters, and learned the ways of the streets.

He was at his lodgings one evening, in a corner by himself reading the newspaper, Caesar lying by his side, when the room fell silent. He looked up to see why the ever-present chatter and banter had ceased. A woman, elegantly dressed, had opened the door and walked into the room, her eyes searching each face.

It was his mother. She had a look of frozen shock that he had seen before—when they had lost everything in Oxford. He hurried to her and brought her to the hallway.

"He's gone, isn't he?" Edgar asked with a mixture of sarcasm and bitterness.

She nodded dimly. "He is dead. And made no provision for me in his will! His sons—his own sons —came to the flat and forced me out on the street. They made me leave my gowns, hats, the jewellery he gave me, books, ornaments, furnishings, my pony and phaeton, everything! All I have is what I'm standing up in, and my reticule, which contains only a few shillings. What hatred they harboured all these years toward me, for their father loved *me* a great deal more than he loved their mother, and they hated me for it. Oh, Edgar, what shall I do now?" she collapsed in his arms, weeping into his shoulder.

"Mother. Stop this. You have to be brave. Look at me —locked up for a crime of which I was an innocent party—" but his mother was not listening. Her entire attention was upon her own predicament. "Mother, I'm earning. I can keep us both. We will get a little flat. Two rooms at least."

"Oh, dearest boy, will you take me back? I am too old now for the dance-floor—I applied there, and they told me there were no vacancies, but I *knew*. I've lost my youth and beauty! Why did Cyril leave me unprovided for? That's two men who have betrayed me! Can I depend upon you, Edgar?"

"Yes, Mother. We are a family, remember?"

It would be a change, living with his mother again. But it was his duty to care for her, to provide for her. And he had hopes that they would get on well, that she would knuckle down and keep house without too much complaining and bitterness. He gave her some money for a decent lodging, and the following evenings were spent hunting for a flat. His mother rejected every one. *'Too noisy, too small, too damp, a horrible smell, overlooking a rough yard,'* etc.

He did not take her with him to Estella Court, and laid down a deposit on a three-room flat there. It was not far from where they had lived before, but was better. An upstairs apartment, where he hoped that his mother would be a little farther from street noise and would be content to employ herself daily in some useful activities undisturbed. He hoped that she would be able to make a cosy home for both of them. Above all, she wanted a servant. A maid-of-all-work, clean and sober and of good morals, who would live out, so he applied to an agency, who sent him a girl who lasted two days before she complained that her mistress was a harridan and she was off. Mrs. Murgatroyd did not take to the next one—*'a coarse girl, very ill-brought up'* and she only lasted hours. The agency threatened that they would send one more only. She was a sweet, obliging girl named Polly, and Mrs. Murgatroyd took a liking to

154

her. She would train her to be a lady's maid, and when they could afford it, they would employ another maid-of-all-work, leaving Polly free to attend to her. They would, of course, move to a larger establishment. Mrs. Murgatroyd was determined to rise again. It would be all up to Edgar!

Edgar settled in as much as he could. But he had to part with Caesar, for his mother would not have him in the flat. He felt bitter about it, but his mother had to come first. Happily, Caesar had friends in the lodging house, and the lads offered to keep him. Edgar reflected that Caesar was much happier there than with a bad-tempered woman who did not like him. It was for the best.

MISS GLENNON

1

867

Clare Glennon was not one of the most popular girls at school—that ranking belonged to the very rich or the very beautiful. But she had three solid, sincere friends. They went about together and as they got older were allowed some freedom outside to go down to the post-office or the shop or to walk in the gardens of Kelsey House, which was not far away. Every year she went home for her holidays, and spent most of those weeks in Fernleigh. Her father insisted she spend at least two weeks of the year with him—her grandmother supported him in this.

Dr. Glennon had bought a large house on the edge of town for his wife and family. They called it 'Glennon

Manor' and had six servants, including a butler to answer the door. His mother reckoned that it was far beyond what he, a country doctor, could afford and that he must be in debt up to his ears.

Anna, now twelve years old, never returned to 23 Raleigh Street, nor had she ever been to Glennon Manor. Her father visited her at her grandmother's home. Her stepmother never came. Clare and Anna had two little step-brothers, Leo and Henry, and she was always busy with them.

Anna had recovered in time from her ordeal at the hands of her stepmother, and was again her cheerful, happy self. Doris was employed solely for her care, and taught her how to lace-crochet, a skill she had learned from her Irish mother. Anna made everything from doilies as gifts for her grandmother, to baby bonnets for poor mothers. Her grandmother was in failing health and Doris was more important to her than anybody else, except Clare, whose return for holidays was eagerly looked forward to by her. Anna still loved dancing and hummed tunes as she took the floor by herself.

Aunt Susanna was in Bengal, and had two children. Clare wrote letters to her and she always wrote back that she was overjoyed to get news from England.

On this sunny June day, Clare and her friends walked down to the shop, for one of the girls needed a new pair of stockings. Their chatter was cheerful and loud, and they were not taking any notice of anything or anybody. They walked along the railway line, and a train came very slowly by, whistling on its last few yards into the station, and a few cheeky young men aboard were hanging out of a window and waving to them, which they were pleased to see, though they pretended to be insulted. A few carriages on, Clare espied a familiar face inside the window—that of Tom, her grandmother's manservant. How curious! She felt anxious so they all turned back, fearing that something had happened at Fernleigh or Glennon Manor.

It was so. Tom was coming to fetch her home, for her grandmother was dying. Clare said a very sorrowful goodbye to her friends, as she knew she would not be back. They were in their last term of schooling. Her box was made ready and Tom escorted her home upon the train.

By the time they arrived, her grandmother had died. Anna was in floods of tears and would not be consoled. And Clare thought at once—*'what is to become of us now? Where do we have to go? I don't want to go back to my father's house—and Anna is not welcome there—! We can hardly go to India! There's nobody else to take us!'*

During the funeral, the thought would not leave her. She observed her father and stepmother at the graveside. Hetty caught her eye and looked away again. Anna was not in attendance. Her father said she was too distraught and left her with Doris.

What would become of them now?

"Where are Anna and I to go, Papa?" she put the question to her father quietly as she contrived to lead him a little away from the group as they reached Fernleigh. A luncheon had been prepared at the house for all the mourners.

He did not reply. She repeated the question, and said:

"Papa, you know my stepmother will not take Anna. What is to become of her? May I live with her in Fernleigh?"

"No. Out of the question, an unprotected young woman like you. You must come to us." His manner went to her heart—for this was uttered in a wooden voice, as if it was a necessary evil to him.

"And—what of Anna, Papa? Will she come too? And Doris?"

He turned to her.

"Leave Anna to me," he said. In a disinterested tone of voice, his manner cold, Clare knew that his second family meant far more to him than his first—his heart, his life, his energies belonged to Hetty and his boys. It was like a sword piercing her breast to hear him speak so.

He was planning to take Anna to the asylum! It had to be. Perhaps she would be better off there than with Hetty, though? No. Father always had said that it was a dreadful place. Would they lock her up, restrain her with belts and ropes? What about her lace-crochet? Would she be allowed a lace hook? Would she even be allowed to dance there?

"It's not the asylum, is it, Papa? You know she will never get used to it. You know—and being twelve years old, she needs particular care—"

He silenced her with a deep frown. Hetty had drawn near, and was giving her a long look, as if suspecting her. Clare averted her eyes.

PLANS

There was a great deal of chatter during lunch, the usual talk at funerals, of relating and updating information about mutual friends and relatives. But Clare kept silent, deep in thought. Anna was not at the table. She was eating with the servants.

After lunch, Clare slipped down to the kitchen and asked Doris if her father had given her any instructions. Doris nodded, and indicated that she wished to speak to her alone, so they went a little way away into a hallway.

"I'm to have her ready to go somewhere at four o'clock. She will not need to take anything with her, which I think very odd indeed! If she's to be boarded out with a village family, she will need clothes and her combs and boots!"

"She's being taken to the asylum, Doris." The old woman crossed herself and uttered a silent prayer. "Unless I can stop it. I have a plan. Please pack her clothes, and her shoes and combs and ribbons, as much as will fit into a carpet bag. And her crochet hooks, and thread if there's room."

After lunch, Clare watched for her father taking the guests to the front door, and signalled her stepmother that she wished to speak to her alone, and so they went into the morning room.

"I have to be very quick before Papa sees the visitors off and comes to look for us. I am to come and live with you today." Clare said.

Her stepmother nodded, and forced a smile.

"So, when I come and live with you, it will be forever, you know. I have no intention of marrying."

Hetty seemed annoyed to hear this. "Of course, you will marry! You have improved greatly over the last year. You have bloom and not a little grace. I already have somebody in mind, a Mr. Nugent—he is still young, at thirty—"

"No, I will refuse him and everybody. And will be a plague to you, I know. Unless I were to disappear, for instance."

Her stepmother regarded her with narrow eyes.

"Disappear? Run away? Just like that?"

"Yes, and this afternoon. With Anna."

"Oh. I see."

"And if we did go away, we would never come back to be a bother to you again, ever. Papa would not have the expense of me, or of Anna at the asylum, and we'd never return."

"I don't want to know anymore," said Mrs. Glennon, raising her hands in a stopping motion. "What do you need?"

"I need money, as much as you can give me, but at least twenty pounds."

"I do not have that sum about me, I can tell you, all I can give you is ten or eleven."

"That and jewellery, then."

"You are greedy."

"No, I'm prudent."

"Wait here," she swished toward the door and returned quickly with something in her hand. Thankfully her father was seeing the mourners to the gate!

"These were your mother's, and it is only right you should have them. Your father will not miss them. And here—eleven pounds, it's all I have." She placed a necklace and some brooches into her hands, and banknotes.

"Thank you," said Clare. "And one more thing—we need your confidence."

"I am not likely to tell your father." The reply was cynical. "Where are you going?"

"I'm not sure yet."

"I'm not a wicked woman, you know." Mrs. Glennon remarked, as if it was very important to leave Clare with this knowledge. "My actions all those years ago were commonplace in many families, and I did not know why everybody took on so at the time, though I have had time to think about it since. I am ashamed of myself now."

"Then I have one other request to make of you." Clara said in a gentler tone. "Please, please do not allow Doris to leave this house without a good character."

Her stepmother nodded. "I will write her one. Please try not to think too evil of me, Clare." She seemed sincere, and Clare felt that she would keep her word.

She had no time to waste. She and Anna had to catch the three o'clock train to London. They could lose themselves there. But, she reflected grimly as she tripped down the back stairs to the kitchen, probably nobody would look for them. She felt very angry and betrayed. Her father had long abandoned them, she felt, and this was only a natural consequence. He would cease to think of them. She remembered the father of her childhood, the happy, gentle, doting Papa! Everything changed when Mama died. But she had no time to think—she had to take Anna and run, out the back gate, over the fields to avoid being seen, until they came to the railway station.

Doris had Anna ready. Clare gave her one of the banknotes for she would be out of a place for a time. She only wished it could be more.

She already felt she knew London. Her schoolfriend Margaret had a brother who was a Crown prosecutor, and he was fond of writing long letters home about the cases he dealt with in court. Swindles, counterfeits, pickpockets. She'd be no stranger to the dark shadows and the criminals lurking in every doorway, and she'd mind her pockets on the omnibuses, and would not let anybody stand near to her, and if someone caught her attention to ask directions, she'd make sure that there was nobody snipping the strings of her reticule on her other side—oh, she knew all the tricks London criminals could get up to! As for Anna, she would never allow her out of her sight.

They arrived in London as darkness fell. Anna did not fully understand that they had left Devon for good, and thought she was on a holiday. She felt excited to see the lights and the bustle of such a place. Clare found them a room in a good boarding house near the railway station. Tomorrow, she'd rent a place where she could begin her little restaurant, and then go to a market to buy pots and pans and a boiler if she could get one cheap. Anna would help her with the work, she was good at simple tasks.

She was sure it would all be very easy.

33

ORGAN GRINDER

awn the following day was slow in coming, for there was a torrential rain. It poured so heavily that Clare did not leave the house except to go out in the afternoon during a short break in the weather. Anna was amusing herself with her crochet, but she longed to get out to see this new world.

Now that she was actually here, in London, Clare's dreams seemed more unreachable than what she had planned at home. For one thing, she was responsible for Anna—childlike Anna, who trusted her absolutely. But first, there had to be sight-seeing and recreation. Clare wanted to see the Crystal Palace, so they went there that afternoon, and were enchanted. But that night, with Anna sleeping peacefully, reality began to sink in.

I don't know how or where to begin this enterprise, she thought, feeling a rising panic. *Our money will run out soon. Everything seemed so easy at home in Devonshire! I would come here, and set up a kitchen, but I have not the faintest idea on how to go about it ... I thought it would all unfold somehow, no—I didn't think about it at all ... I just wanted to get Anna away.*

She lay awake all night. A part of her wished to run back to the known, to Devonshire, even to Glennon Manor to Papa and Hetty, and live there, but then she thought of Anna—no, it would not be. She would not condemn Anna to a life devoid of humanity and love—*'put away'*! She had to stay, had to do something. She would buy a newspaper tomorrow and look at the advertisements.

She slipped out of the house early and purchased the daily newspaper. Quickly she perused the advertisements. Property for rent—with a jolt, she realised that everything—just everything—would be far too expensive. Besides she did not even know if these places were suitable for her purpose. She would have to look around on foot.

After they had dressed and eaten breakfast, they set off on an omnibus. They had never ridden in one before, and Anna was jumping with excitement. The young woman entering the bus ahead of them had a wide crinoline. As she squeezed through the narrow door her compressed hoop raised her hem, putting her in danger of displaying ankles and petticoats, but the conductor held her skirt down, grinning and remarking that 'he was a married man,' which caused titters and tut-tuts, both. *People are different here*, Clare thought, as the owner of the crinoline gave him a saucy smile without as much as a blush on her face. But she had forgotten her anxieties for a moment and was as amused as Anna, who was hiding her glee behind hands tightly held over her mouth.

They sat beside a mother and child. The little boy immediately set up a wail after he dropped a penny on the straw-covered floor. Anna scrambled to help him look for it and held it up, delighted, to the entire bus before she dropped it into his palm. Thereafter, she gazed out the window, her eyes fixed upon all that was passing outside, tugging at Clare's sleeve to draw her attention to everything she saw.

Clare was not so enthralled—her responsibility weighed heavily upon her and again, she felt she had taken on too much, for she knew nothing of how to start a business. Everything she beheld that was new and strange caused a stab of anxiety, and she felt as if she and Anna had landed in a foreign country.

Londoners had a quick, forward air, a sense of determination and purpose, a shrewdness about their surroundings. Clare did not feel equal to them.

The omnibus brought them to an area named Whitechapel, and they were spilled onto a busy street. Clare felt that they had stumbled onstage into a pantomime with everybody around them in costume, shouting their lines all together. "Pretty pansies, all a-blowing!" cried the flower seller, with billowing apron and carrying a colourful basket. A butcher's boy carried his load of meat upon his shoulder, and though small, pushed through the crowd like a little prize-fighter. A milkman, in his tall pot hat and white smock, drove two cows along, "New milk!" was his call, and children ran from their houses with jugs. Shoppers stood at windows; walked in all directions, or crossed the road, giving a penny to the crossing-sweep who swept rubbish out of their path. Added to this mob were several wagons making their way through, one held casks of beer, another was piled with furniture and a family sitting on top moving to a new home.

Anna was mesmerised, her eyes wide with wonder. Clare felt overwhelmed. Everybody here had a part to play in the life of this bustling city—but what was hers? Every house on the street was a shop—bakers, butchers, grocers, old clothes vendors, pawnshops, gin shops—where would she fit in? New and shy, doubts assailed her again.

'It's too much for now', she said, finding herself shrinking from her vague dream of renting a kitchen and serving food. She did not have the faintest idea how to begin.

"Baked potatoes!" rang the cry from a youth juggling his wares in a wooden box. An idea occurred to Clare. After they had secured a room, she could buy two dozen potatoes, boil them over the fire, and take them out and sell them—what could be simpler? The same for pies, pastry and meat filling—all in good time! *Start small*, she told herself, in a burst of inspiration.

Getting a room was harder than she thought, and for a very painful reason. The landlords or landladies looked at Anna and shook their heads. One even went so far as to remark in a loud whisper: *"There are places for those people, you know."* Clare hurried Anna away, but there was no doubt that she had not only heard but understood the meaning.

"Where are those places, Clare?"

"She meant—schools."

"She seemed a bit mean though. Why are some people mean, Clare?"

"Some don't follow God's law to love everybody."

"Like Mother Hetty," said Anna. "We should stay away from those people, Clare."

"You are a wise one," Clare said, warmly, giving her sister a hug. Quietly, she wondered if perhaps she should go alone to find a room. Once she had the key, and she and Anna had settled in, landlords would see that she was a beautiful, sweet girl with a lovely nature, and not what they feared her to be, whatever that was.

She saw a sign with '*room for rent*' on the door of an old building, and very reluctantly decided to leave Anna around the corner. There was an organ grinder there and many children were jumping and dancing about.

"Wait here for me," she said to her. "Don't go anywhere, and don't let anybody tempt you away— do you understand?"

Anna nodded, her eyes upon the organ grinder and his monkey, while Clare ran to the house, was taken up to the furnished room, decided it was suitable and paid her deposit. She was given keys. Phew!

Thank God, they had a place at last, to start their new life! She felt instantly more confident.

When she went around the corner again, she saw a larger group of people than before, and they were gathered in a circle, laughing heartily. The organ grinder was playing and in the middle of the circle, she saw Anna, dancing to the music.

"There's nothing as funny as seeing an idiot dance!" said one woman, wiping tears of laughter from her eyes. Clare gave her a look of disgust, then pushed through the circle and took Anna by the arm.

"Come on, Anna, that's enough. We have to go now."

"But look, Clare, I earned money!" she bent to pick up pennies and halfpennies that had been thrown on the ground at her feet.

The show was over, the crowd dispersed. Anna seemed oblivious that her dancing had attracted anything other than joy in the onlookers, and had thankfully missed the fact that she had been the object of ridicule. Clare helped her to pick up the change from the ground. They gave the organ grinder half.

"The monkey is sad," remarked Anna as they went home.

"Why do you say that?"

"I know he's sad."

Anna remarked things that nobody else saw.

But Anna could not brood for long. "Look, that's three pennies, five half-pennies, and five farthings!" She built them into little columns later as Clare was setting the room to rights.

Clare drew the curtains over the dismal view outside, a squalid yard with piles of rusty iron and scrap metal, and lit the lamp. The kettle was on the boil over the fire and for supper, they were having beef pies and potatoes and bread. She saw Anna's smile of contentment. She was safe. Thank God! She had done the right thing after all!

34

ANNA SAVES THE DAY

T he girls went to the High Street the following day, where Clare bought a second-hand copper saucepan and a wicker basket.

"Now for the potatoes, are you coming, Anna?"

Anna was dawdling, gazing at a little doll, so Clare, in a burst of generosity, bought it for her. Her name was to be Lily.

They wandered among the vegetable stalls, and Clare purchased two dozen potatoes to take home and cook. It was Saturday, and she knew that the markets would come to life later with shoppers for Sunday.

"You must be a big family, Ma'am," said the vegetable seller.

"No, I'm going to cook them and sell them hot. But not around here," she added hastily. "Nearer to where we live."

The woman said nothing, but took the money and gave her change. As Clare walked on, she was joined by a young woman who said to her:

"I 'eard what you said! You're new 'ere, aren't you? You shouldn't buy the potatoes in the market. You should get them from a grower! A farmer! You won't make no profit, you won't!"

"Where am I to find a farmer?"

"In the country!" said the girl, astounded at the ignorance, before she disappeared into the throngs.

The girl was correct. She did not sell any cooked potatoes that night until she had drastically reduced the price, causing her to sell at a loss. This was disheartening. She'd have to find a farmer! Preferably somebody who would be coming to town regularly and who would deliver, for she could surely not go out the country, and haul sacks of potatoes back. She had to find out what the other sellers did.

Clare knew that she had to combat her natural reticence in this new, bold world if she was to be successful. Thankfully, necessity overcame it. She was determined not to be hurt if she was met with rebuffs or ridicule. The first two vegetable sellers she met smirked as if they had to give away the secret password to Her Majesty's Treasury, and she moved on, but she swallowed her pride and went on to the next one, a rather fat women in a large hat wreathed with ribbons, bows, fruit and birds' eggs. This time, Anna, who did not have a shy bone in her body, pre-empted her, and without even knowing how to compliment somebody in order to obtain a favour, exclaimed.

"Missus, I like your hat! Is that a real pear?"

"Oh no, dearie, not real. And the birds' eggs aren't real neither. What can I do fer you?"

Again, Anna pre-empted her older sister.

"We want to know where to get potatoes, and they don't know!" she pointed up the street. "Do you know, please?"

"We're just arrived in town, and need to set up a stall," Clare explained, putting one arm about her sister in her usual affectionate gesture, while Anna beamed at the lady in the hat. "We have no means of support, and have to make our own way."

"What, just the two of you?"

Clare nodded.

"Spitalfields. The Market isn't far from 'ere. Go there of a Saturday afore three o'clock, and you'll see the farmers come in to sell. You'll know them by the carts and the horses, big dray ones, and drive a bargain, they expect it, and then place a regular order with one of 'em."

35

NEAR-DESPAIR

After doing what was suggested, if Clare thought her greatest hurdle was over, she was very wrong. She was all ready to sell hot baked potatoes and had picked a good spot beside a public house. But when she went there alone at five o'clock one evening, she found the coveted spot taken by a man and woman selling leeks and cabbages.

I'll just stand a little way off, she thought, disappointed. But after a few minutes they bellowed at her to leave.

"Be off! We pay for this space," the man shouted. "You've no right to be 'ere."

"Pay! Pay who?"

"Pay who!" the woman laughed out loud, a hoarse, unkind laugh. "Be off with you!"

Clare stood her ground until the man rushed over, picked up three potatoes and dashed them on the ground. "Now will you be off?"

She backed away, almost in tears.

Clare was almost robbed of all of her will to sell by this nasty encounter, but necessity meant she had to keep going. If all the spots on the the pavements were rented, what was she to do? So she kept walking, and soon found that if she did not keep crying her wares like the other sellers, trying to shout louder, she did not get any attention. By nine, she was hoarse, but had sold some potatoes—cold by now of course, so she had to reduce the price.

"This is almost too difficult," she said to herself. "I wonder if I could get a job as a cook instead, but then if they would not take Anna—?"

She struggled. Anna stayed in their room now, rather than be dragged all over the East End, for she had not the strength, and coughed. Clare feared for her safety all day long, although she had instructions not to leave the room or to answer the door to anybody. The days were getting shorter and the coal fires were making the air smoky. Anna coughed when she was outside, and yet she did not want to be inside, and worse—alone all day long. She began to complain and Clare began to be short with her. Anna did not know that she was the reason that they had come to London, and though Clare never told her of her Papa's plan for her, she harboured resentment when Anna got difficult and argued that she wanted to go out, making life even more difficult than it was already.

"I don't want to hear anything else about it," she scolded her one evening, after Anna had greeted her in tears, saying she was tired of London and when were they going back home?

"You're getting like—like Mother Hetty," said Anna. "Always cross!"

The comparison made Clare startle. *Like Mother Hetty!*

"I am sorry, Anna," she said, embracing her warmly. "I have money worries, and it's making me short of temper. We can't go home, love. We'd have to live with Mother Hetty if we did. We may have to move from here into a cheaper room."

"It's all right," Anna said, cheering again, buttoning the dress on her doll. "Lily says it's all right."

There had to be some way she could earn money and take Anna to work with her. But for the moment, there was no help for it.

One October evening, she had no luck at all, and sat down on a doorstep almost in tears. She laid her basket by her feet. As she did, she saw an old woman pass by, and trip on an uneven part of the pathway, falling down. She jumped up and together with other passers-by, helped the woman up. She was not hurt, just shaken and with many thanks, she went upon her way.

When Clare turned around to the steps again, she saw that her basket was gone. She looked around desperately, but saw nobody with her basket, and rightly concluded that it was gone for good, together with her potatoes that were to pay the rent. All her jewellery was in pawn. It was too much—she flopped down upon the steps and with her head against the railing, wept.

"What's the matter? Can I help?" Another woman who had helped the victim approached. She was in her thirties and her eyes were kind.

Clare told her, in bursts of sobbing.

"You have a West Country accent!" was the woman's response. "Are you from Devon or Cornwall, perhaps?"

Clare brightened up—somebody who knew Devonshire! Not only who knew it, but was from there, as was evidenced by the woman's next words. But even more wonderful—this woman said that she was from *Fernleigh*!

"My name is Davey," she said warmly.

The name rang a bell with Clare—she had heard the name, sometime before.

"Mine is Glennon," she said. "Clare Glennon."

"Come with me back to my lodging," urged Miss Davey. "It's not far, and I'm sure you'd like a cup of tea."

"Thank you, but I can't. I have to get back to my sister. She is a simpleton, poor girl, and I don't like to leave her for long. She hates being left alone."

"If you do not live faraway, then we can call for her. How came you to be in London?"

Clare sighed. "It's a long story, our mother died. Our father remarried, but our new stepmother did not want Anna. Our father—he changed—especially when our stepmother gave him two sons—and so here we are, alone."

"It is a sad story—but all too common."

"My grandmother was against the marriage. She thought that Papa was acting too hastily after the loss of our mother. She didn't like the Sheltons—that is my stepmother's maiden name."

"Sheltons!" cried Miss Davey, stopping short in amazement.

"Yes—are you acquainted with them?"

"Yes, I am. They are relatives. No, don't be upset you mentioned them. Your grandmother was correct to mistrust them. I and my brother have been greatly injured by the Shelton family."

At that, Clare remembered her grandmother's history of the young Daveys who had been cheated of their inheritance by Hetty's parents.

"So you are Caroline Davey!"

They had reached the apartment, and Miss Davey was introduced to Anna, who took a great liking to her without delay as she had a pretty hat, and introduced her to her doll and showed her her crochet.

"Come to my lodging and find some other work." Miss Davey said to Clare. "We'll find something for you to do in the kitchen, and if Anna does not wish to stay in the kitchen with you, she can come and sit in my shop—I'm a milliner."

"Milliner means hats!" cried Anna. "I love hats!"

"Perhaps you can make lace flowers for our hats," Miss Davey said warmly. "From what I have seen here, you could earn money for your work."

After Miss Davey left, Clare got on her knees and thanked God for this blessing. Her day had begun in a horrible way, and had gone from bad to worse. She reflected that if she had not left the steps to help the poor old woman, she and Miss Davey would never have met. God works in mysterious ways.

MISS DAVEY'S STORY

T he lodging house that Miss Davey stayed in was a cheerful, plain place in a quiet alley away from the High Street. Clare and Anna were given a room to themselves. Clare feared that the other women would not accept Anna in their midst, and if that were the case, then she would be forced to move again.

Happily, Miss Davey was held in esteem among the residents and that smoothed the way and ended any doubts that the women had. But Clare saw the doubts on some faces.

Why do people think, she asked herself sadly, *that simpletons like my little sister have a tendency to be unpredictable and dangerous? It's so wrong!*

Anna soon won hearts. Her happy smile was for everybody. She gave compliments because she said aloud what she genuinely thought—Miss Jones had nice curls, Miss Armstrong had nice flowers on her apron, Miss Craig's lace was snowy-white.

Clare quickly got into her new work. She was to be paid three shillings a week plus her bed and board. It was a relief to have a regular income.

Street-selling was not for me, she thought, a little ruefully. *Perhaps you have to be brought up to it. I never was able to push my way past other people and my voice was too soft to be heard over the thousand different shouts in the London streets!*

On her first night in her new lodging, she was awakened by the noise of revelry in the early hours of the morning. Had the revellers just come in, she wondered? Then she simply turned over and thought no more about it, thinking that this was normal for Whitechapel.

Anna went to the millinery shop every day, and sat in the back working her lace-crochet. She made beautiful roses for the hats. She occasionally met the customers, if they expressed admiration and curiosity as to the craftswoman. Many were astounded to see that she was of a simple mind and yet could make beautiful items. Miss Davey did not lose any customers because of Anna.

Many women at Bethany Lodging for Women slept late, and the downstairs hall often had only a few women for breakfast. All were present for the main meal at one o'clock, and most were there for supper. After supper, the hall turned into a relaxing place, with a big fire, gossip, the browsing of fashion magazines, endless cups of tea, sewing and laundry and the hanging of wet clothes at the far end of the room on washing lines.

Clare wondered about the women who dressed up and went out at night. She saw these women wear rouge and powder and paint their lips. They wore clothes that were fashionable but saucy, low cut in the front and short enough to show ankles. She asked Miss Davey about this. "Where is there to go, so late?" she asked them one evening, over a cup of tea. "And some of them come home full of merriment!"

Miss Davey looked down at her plate. "They are unfortunates," she said.

"You mean—?" Clare was shocked beyond belief. *Miss Davey had brought her to a house with prostitutes living there! What did this mean?*

"Unfortunates?" She repeated. She had heard her father refer to this woman or that as an *'unfortunate'* but had not found out the meaning until she was at school.

"Yes, I mean that."

"How did it come to be that women like that live in a respectable place like this?" asked Clare, struggling with her own feelings. Would she have to take Anna away?

"They have nowhere else to live. And—they are trying, all of them, to give up the life, but find they cannot do it—yet. We don't allow gin or any other alcoholic drink here, but they do imbibe while they are out. Of course, no men are allowed in here."

Clare was silent.

"Do you think badly of me for bringing you here? For I had no ill intentions, Clare."

"No, Miss Davey," said Clare, astonished. "You are as pure as the driven snow, as my grandmother would have put it."

Miss Davey gave a smile, but it was a sad one, and she changed the subject.

"Anna is getting on so well at the milliners," she said. "Does she say she's happy there?"

"Oh yes, she loves it. She can see people passing up and down the alley and hear the conversation in the shop—our Anna was made for company."

But the other matter had not left Clare's mind.

"Miss Davey, are you running a shelter for fallen women?" she asked in a low tone, for some women had settled themselves with tea at the other end of the table, and Anna was having her hair brushed by a women named Bess not far away.

"Yes, you might say so," Miss Davey looked at her, and Clare saw tears glisten in her eyes. "I want to make good come out of the evil that—that happened to me."

Clare's eyes had an astonished look, but Miss Davey's obvious distress made her pull herself up and say,

"I do not want to pry, Miss Davey. You have done my sister and I a great service and came to our rescue also," she smiled with affection.

"I'm going to tell you my story," Miss Davey said. "Because you know now, I'm sure, that I was one of *them*, once." She took a deep breath. "My brother and

I arrived, here having been thrown out of our home by the Sheltons—that part you know, how it came about. We moved in with an aunt and uncle in Cheapside, and were happy there. They were to be responsible for us. I was fifteen years old, and my brother two years older.

"One summer evening, we went to the pleasure grounds at Surrey Gardens. It was a delightful scene. But near the time for us to come home, I wandered away to see something that held my curiosity. I turned to go back to my party, and saw a man blocking my path. So I quickly took another path, and then left by a back gate. I became completely lost, finding that I had left the Gardens behind me. I kept walking. I descended to a very low area, the like of which I had not seen before. But there was a door open in a house, and I saw a woman inside—so with a feeling of great relief I knocked and entered and spoke to her, telling her that I was lost. She asked me my name and I gave it—I said I was staying with my aunt and uncle in Cheapside. She was very clever. She asked me their name—and I gave it—she said she knew my aunt very well. She had done sewing for her only last year. I was so relieved—what great luck! She said that as it was so late, I should stay the night in her house and then she would take me back first thing in the morning. She gave me a nice room, came in with a drink of milk and waited while I drank it. I did not really want it, but I did not wish to appear ungrateful for this kindness that she was showing me."

Miss Davey paused and wiped a tear from her eye.

"The milk was drugged. I remember no more, except —I awoke in the morning—and knew I had been—I had been ruined."

Clare was horrified.

"What happened next?" she asked gently.

"I was kept prisoner in that house for weeks and suffered many different—" she could not go on, and covered her eyes. "I met with no more kindness from that woman. She and the men she brought in broke my spirit. After three months, I was a different person. I could have, later, found my way back to my aunt and uncle, but what could they have done with me? I was utterly ruined. There was no hope, no future for me except what that evil woman wished. I worked for her. I saw the same thing happen to other girls, in those cases lured away with promises of honest employment. So you see, I was quite worried when I met you, and your sister—I wanted to be sure you were both safe for there are many like her about."

"For that I am very grateful, Miss Davey." Clare laid a hand on her shoulder.

"What happened to you then?" she asked after a silence.

"After some years, I met a great Christian lady who helped me. She did not judge me! She owns this house and the shop. The shop doesn't make much money, and without her patronage, we could not have this shelter. I suppose that what I have said has shocked you, Clare. Did you believe, before now, that there was such evil in the world?"

"No, not evil like that, no. What happened to her, the woman?"

"When I got the courage, I went to the police. They investigated her. They found two missing girls with her. Like me, they had been broken in spirit, unable to believe that anything would change, that anybody would believe or listen to them. She was transported for twenty years."

"Why do you not write to your aunt and uncle?" Clare asked with some earnestness after another moment. "What if they died, not knowing what happened to you? And what of your brother?"

"I've often thought of writing, but I hesitate. My brother is most likely married, and there'd be scandal. At the time of the trial, my name wasn't mentioned, and charges were brought on behalf of the younger girls because those crimes were more recent."

"Please do let them know where you are, and that you are all right! Your brother will be happy to know you are alive and well. As for his wife, if she loves him, she'll be happy too, and welcome you. I believe in loyalty and love." Clare wondered, even as she spoke, if she really believed this. Why had her father all but abandoned them, especially Anna?

Miss Davey lifted her head and smiled.

"You've convinced me. I shall do exactly that."

They began to speak of other matters, and as Clare was falling asleep that night, it occurred to her that she ought to let her father know that she and Anna were safe. But what if he came to London, looking for them? She did not want that. He had the power to remove Anna from her. No, she could not risk it.

EDGAR'S TROUBLE

"Edgar!" the voice drifted out from the outer room. "I need ten shillings."

"Mother, I haven't got two shillings, not to mind ten."

"Why not, Edgar?"

Edgar sighed in frustration as he dragged a comb through his hair. It was early morning, and he had been up half the night with stomach pain. But he had to go to work.

"Because I don't get paid until Saturday. Then we have to pay rent, and pay Polly and Edie," he shouted.

"There is no need to shout, and let all the neighbours know our business," was the reply. Then there was a silence, a sullen silence that Edgar was very familiar with.

"Why can't you get a better position?" complained Mrs. Murgatroyd, standing at the door. Edgar wanted to stop his ears. His mother would never understand that his fraud conviction barred him from advancing to the coveted office work, the work that would bring him connections, which would in turn raise him in society, which would somehow end up in a seat in Parliament. She hated that he worked in Halley's Shipyard, and told her neighbours that he was an engineer there, and that Mr. Halley had taken a great liking to him. None of them believed her.

He disliked his work too, but there was, for the present, no way out, although he did remind himself he was part of a team that produced a beautiful vessel, and he was always proud to look at the new ship when she was all painted up, rigged out and ready for sea-trials. Of course he'd like to be in the grand offices of Halley Shipbuilding—it might have happened had he been able to continue his schooling, but it would never happen now, and he had to be content with his menial but important part in her construction, riveting the large metal plates to the outside of the hull.

His mother did nothing all day long except play Patience with a deck of cards. She still fancied herself a lady. She ate a great deal and took no exercise, so she was becoming very overweight. Her cooking skills had not improved. Undercooked pork, or chicken tough as leather, and watery vegetables were Edgar's lot after a hard day's work. He developed a stomach complaint that made him double up in pain and be unable to eat for several days together. He was becoming very thin.

"Where is Polly?" his mother twitched the curtain to see if she was coming up the street. "I can't stand unpunctuality in a servant."

"Bye, Mother." Edgar made his escape. He reached the shipyards just on time to sign in before the foreman took away the book. He joined the other men on the gantry.

That evening, he found his mother in a very bad mood. Polly had not come. Mrs. Murgatroyd in her impatience had put on her hat and cloak and walked to her home to find out why she had not come to work.

"Her mother answered the door," she said to Edgar. "And she said that she'd just been informed out *what*

I was, and if she'd known, she said, *'I'd never have let my daughter darken your doorstep!'*—her very words! What an insult, Edgar! Everybody has used me so ill! If I did not have you, Edgar, I would die. I was so distraught I could not do any shopping, and I don't trust Edie with money, so there's yesterday's cold tongue and a pear."

"Mother, I can't take fruit at the moment. Did I not tell you?"

"Oh. I forgot." She sat beside the fire. "I do not know what to do now for a lady's maid," she said. "I detest my life, Edgar. I'm in such poor spirits, you cannot possibly imagine the depths to which I fall when you're out. Everything was stolen from us, and we have no redress."

"Did Uncle Evelyn die yet?" Edgar asked wickedly, to rally her spirits. "And if he dies, does his attorney-at-law know where to find you?"

"What if we removed to Switzerland, Edgar? He's spending the remainder of his days there, it seems."

Edgar looked in the bread bin. "Mother, we have no bread. What am I to eat if there's no bread?" he asked in annoyance. "And what of breakfast tomorrow?"

"*Let them eat cake,*" said Mrs Murgatroyd to nobody in particular. Edgar sighed in frustration.

"I'm going out for bread," he said to her. He left the room and took the stairs quickly. He was angry.

DR. LUDLOW

E dgar was missing days from work. The pain in his stomach was so bad that he could hardly get up in the mornings. His mother seemed not to understand this.

"Please, Mother, send Edie for the doctor, or I shall die."

This must have alarmed her, for an hour later, a doctor was bending over his bed, prodding his abdominal area, asking if it hurt here, or there, or over here?

"You have severe inflammation of your stomach," he concluded. "You must eat only a very little, and that has to be soft food."

"I can't eat, if she does not prepare it. I can't work. I'm afraid I shall have to apply to the Parish for relief."

The doctor gave him the name of the relieving officer. It was humiliating to go and beg from the Board of Guardians, a group of middle-aged men with bulging waistcoats, all sitting around a mahogany table in the workhouse meeting room. His father had been on the Board of Guardians at Oxford.

"You say your mother is having nervous troubles. Would she wish to have an occupation? We have a vacancy for a nurse in the women's section of the workhouse. Work is good for women who have nervous fancies, is it not, Matron?"

The only woman present nodded vigorously. "That's why we have no nerves here," she said proudly. "The inmates are kept too busy to think about being melancholy or nervous. They are busy from the time they open their eyes until they shut them at night. Idleness of mind and body is not tolerated."

The Chairman of the Board wrote something on a slip of paper.

"Tell her she is to present herself here next Monday at eight o'clock. I do not see why we should provide relief when your mother is able-bodied."

When he went home and told his mother, she was beyond horrified. "Will I go to prison if I don't turn up?" she wanted to know.

"Maybe. But they feed you in prison."

"I had better go, then. I will be mixing with such low people!"

Edgar could not believe his ears. For a time, his mother was going to support *him*! He could rest all day in the quiet flat, not hearing her endless complaining. Edie could prepare his food. It was to be very simple until the pain subsided, thin gruels and soft white bread.

Mrs. Murgatroyd got up early on Monday morning, and complaining bitterly about her lot, attired herself well, and walked to the workhouse to take up her new position. Edgar wondered how she would stand it. Would she be home by noon? He waited, hearing Big Ben strike the hours. But the clock was now striking one, and two ...

To his great surprise, the day wore on, and at about eight o'clock his mother came back. He waited for the complaints, and for her to say that one day was enough, and that she would never go back there again, not for her life. But she did not. Edgar made a cup of tea and they drank it together.

"Are you not going to tell me about it?" he asked at last.

"I detested it for an hour. Then Dr. Ludlow came in —such a gentleman. He saw of course that I'm not the usual class of woman he meets with within those walls. I told him of my misfortune in life, and how I had come to this. He's a bachelor."

Edgar almost choked on his tea.

"So you plan on returning there tomorrow?" he ventured.

"Of course! The last nurse kept a very untidy log, all blobs. I will show them. And the workhouse attendants are slatterns. I will show them too."

"But what do you know of nursing, Mother?" he asked.

"Oh Edgar, Dr. Ludlow has offered to teach me nursing. Is he not a charming man? Don't be surprised, Edgar, if I shall be Mrs. Ludlow very soon."

"Aren't you rather jumping the gun, Mother?"

"Silly Edgar!" she reached over and ruffled his hair.

"And is Dr. Ludlow—an older gentleman?"

"Oh no, Edgar. He is not thirty."

Edgar thought that if a comet were to suddenly leap across the night sky, he could not marvel at it as much as his mother's sudden change of mood. Suddenly, her world was bright.

"I ate a good dinner there, and supper too," she added.

39

NO DITHERERS NEED APPLY

Clare almost wished she had not urged Miss Davey to contact her relations, for as soon as they found out, they swept her up into their arms and back into their lives. Their joy was unbounded. Miss Davey left her millinery shop and the lodging house and would thereafter be under the protection of her brother.

Without her, the Glennons' position in the lodging house altered. Bess wanted Clare's kitchen job, and a few other women began a subtle campaign to evict them as they did not meet the criterion for lodging there and they had friends who wanted places. They began to make both girls uncomfortable. Anna missed the millinery shop, for Gladys, who had taken Caroline's place, did not want her there.

Clare knew that she had to find work. But this time, she would be very wise and plan it carefully.

For some time now she had passed a small chop-house near the docks in the borough of Gullseye very close to a watchman's station. A warm place because of his brazier, it attracted people to stop and warm their hands in winter, and while they were there, the aroma from Mrs. Burns's chop-house reached their nostrils. Clare often stopped there for a cup of tea, but more so because she became friendly with Mrs. Burns and hoped to learn from her. She had no time to lose. London itself impelled her forward—its bustling, impatient air told her that it would not hand anything to her—or wait for her— she had to go out and hunt down what she wanted. London had no use for ditherers. When Mr. Grimes, the watchman, told her that Mrs. Burns was retiring to live with her daughter in St. Albans, she saw the possibilities.

"I'd love to set up a chop-house," she said to Mrs. Burns that very day, her hands around a tankard of tea. "I love cooking, always have."

"Mr. Grimes told you I was retiring, didn't he? Do you want this place?"

"Yes, I do," said Clare.

"I don't own it, I pay rent. I'll put in a good word for you with Mr. Haldane. Would you like to see my little kitchen?"

Clare did not need a second invitation. The kitchen was small indeed, but it had a window, a stove and a counter, shelves and pots and pans, and a little table.

"I get my potatoes from a grower in Lambeth, and my meats from Mr. Percy in Merchant Street hard by. He does 'is own slaughter and it's always fresh as can be."

Clare became more and more eager about the prospect of running her own little food business. Anna could help her, and sit in the restaurant and crochet also. It was a very run-down area that time had passed by, but the daytime would be safe enough for both of them—and Mr. Grimes was always there.

"I'd need to get us a room near," Clare said to Mrs. Burns.

"Bless me, child, my room's in a lovely little house, with very nice people. I'll put in a good word for you."

"Will they accept my sister?" Clare asked bluntly. Mrs. Burns hesitated.

"I'll ask the landlady," she said.

The following week, Mrs. Burns told Clare that the landlady intended to raise the rent after she had gone. "She said she'd been meaning to raise it for a long time but didn't on account of my being there so long," she explained, not meeting her eye, while Clare nodded, knowing the true situation. She was hurt and angry for Anna's sake.

Never mind—she would find a room for them. But to her surprise, Anna found new accommodation. One of the former customers, Mrs. Foote, at the milliner's had become fond of her, and Clare and Anna met her one day walking down Merchant Street.

"We're moving house soon," Anna said after the greetings were over. "We're looking for a room with a window on the street, cos we like to look out. Do you know any place?"

"It's good you asked, Anna! For my brother has a house in Lydia Court, and he told me only this morning that there's a room vacant! A lovely room, sunny in the morning, newly wallpapered, and on the ground floor."

Claire had misgivings about the ground floor, but it seemed so apt, so timely, and solved their problem so easily that she made no objection. When she saw the room, she was very pleased indeed, for it was large and comfortable; there were a table and chairs as well as a large bed, a wardrobe and dressing table and everything was supplied except bedsheets and towels and their coal.

Mr. Haldane agreed to rent out the chop-house to her. It was very reasonable as it was in a derelict spot, between the coal quay and a merchant quay, beside a run-down warehouse. It jutted out onto Lanyard Lane at an awkward angle, robbing passers-by of half the pathway. Dockyard hands, coalmen, sailors, and shipbuilding labour had to pass it on Lanyard Lane to get to Merchant Street, the main route from the aforementioned quays. In Tudor times Gullseye had been a fishing village, but the City had gradually encircled it. At some point it had acquired wharves and a landing stage, but now they were old and rotting in places. Gullseye had escaped London's Great Fire and still had many wooden structures. They were damp in winter and tinder in summer. The people who had been there for generations loved it and would not dream of living anywhere else, old as it was.

The date for taking over the chop-house was fixed upon, and Clare could hardly wait to hold the key in her hands. She saw any challenges ahead to be mild ones, and she did not see how anything could stand in her way of success. If she had foreseen the difficulties and evils, she would not have been so enthralled, for the notorious Scarlet Swords gang had just run the Scuttler Blues off that part of the quays and were about to let everybody know.

40

DASHED HOPE

M rs. Murgatroyd came home one evening day and was quite miserable.

"Are you better yet, Edgar? I can't go on."

"Mother, I thought you loved your work!"

His mother's silence and disgusted look told him otherwise.

"What happened?"

"Dr. Ludlow is getting married."

"Oh."

"The cad! He led me on, he did. Paid me so much attention, that I thought he was in love with me. But it was not so. This woman he's marrying is the daughter of the beadle, so you know they have it all wrapped up between them. And I'm tired of dirty linen and the bad air and smells of the infirmary. When are you going back to work?"

"Never fear, Mother, I will look for a job tomorrow."

Edgar could not endure a day of constant complaining of how ill his mother was being used, so he resolved to go and look for work. His position had not been held for him. He was very thin and his eyes were hollow. He had a fruitless day and all they had to eat that evening was tea and bread and a few herrings.

SCARLET SWORDS

The Devon Chop-House was up and running. Clare served mutton chops and blood pudding and sausages, rashers, fried fish, potatoes and beans. There was bread and butter in abundance, and lashings of hot tea and coffee. It had a sawdust floor, two big tables with wooden forms each side and a chair at each end. The cups and plates were plain, dull pewter, and the lamps were the smelly spermaceti oil, until she could afford better. It was a man's place, and Clare at first bit her lip at some of the language she was hearing, and wondered if she should put a sign up, *No Swearing* but decided with resignation that it would drive away her best customers—hungry sailors and dockworkers. Anna soon dropped a bad word or two and Clare scolded her. Unfortunately, she let one drop herself one day when she burned a saucepan and endured the same from Anna as she had given to her, and they ended up in gales of laughter.

Anna helped peel the potatoes and wash dishes, and otherwise sat and did her own work—lace roses— which she, unprompted by Clare, offered for sale to anybody, "for your sweetheart's hat." She charged threepence and soon had a tidy stack piled up on her little work-table in the back.

They were making a little money, and Clare was thrilled at her success, making the long days worth the trouble, for she had to stay open until ten o'clock. She did not like the docks at night, and though Anna pleaded to be allowed to go home before she did, she couldn't leave the business to take her home and she couldn't close to take her home, for the stove was inclined to overheat and she was afraid of a fire. This old hut would go up like a firework. Anna got very tired sometimes and fell asleep with her head on her folded arms like a small child. Clare did not know what to do. Find a room nearer? And if she left to take her home, she, Clare would have to walk home alone.

One day she saw that there was a young man lounging near her premises. He was rough-looking, with a scarlet hat and cravat. He wore a black velveteen jacket that had seen better days and worsted trousers and thick boots. She asked Mr. Grimes if he had noticed him.

"Aye, he's from the Scarlet Swords. They run things around 'ere after dark."

This made her even more nervous. One day, she saw the youth cross over toward the chop-house and her heart sank when he entered.

"May I help you?" she asked politely, noting that he was looking around with arrogance instead of meeting her eye.

"You're newly opened?" he asked.

"Yes, just a short time ago. We serve mutton chops today, with mashed potatoes, all just ready, take a seat."

"Don't want no vittles."

"Tea then? Coffee?"

"No, I've come to discuss business with regard to this premises."

"I rent this premises, if you have business, you must discuss it with my landlord."

"No, this business is with you, keep your landlord out of it. I owns this area, see?"

"No, I don't see."

"All the businesses in this here area, Lanyard Street up to Barring Green, pays me to keep their shops open."

Clare could hardly believe this. She was about to be sarcastic and ask him if Halley's Shipyard was beholden to him, but decided that this was not a good idea. The look in this fellow's eye was hard and humourless.

"I never heard of that system," Clare ventured. "Are you working for the City, then?"

"Are you trying to be funny?"

"No, not at all—but this is my first business and I suppose I don't know all the rules."

"Here's the rule. You pay me money, and me and my friends, we'll see you come to no 'arm. We'll bully for you."

"Bully for me?"

"Aye. Guard this business, and you."

Many things ran through Clare's head. It would be good to have a protector—but not a gang member! But how to get out of this without incurring his ill-will? And what of the dark winter nights, if she did not do as he said, could she put herself and Anna in danger?

"How much money?"

"Five shillings a week."

Five shillings a week! That was preposterous.

"I can't give you that much. Leave it with me, and I'll see what I can do." Her heart was hammering in her chest. She could see the outline of a knife under his coat.

"I'll be back soon, so don't forget. You don't want your little sister to get lost, do you? I know where you live."

Miss Davey's ordeal shot through Clare's mind. She began to tremble, and tried to control it.

After he had left, Clare exhaled deeply and sat at a table. She was shaking.

"Who was that?" asked Anna, appearing from the kitchen. "What did he say about me getting lost?"

"He was saying to take care, and he'd protect us. But I didn't take to him, Anna. He's not nice."

"Don't pay him anything. I won't get lost, Clare."

THE DAMSEL'S KINDLY ACT

The following day saw Clare fearful of a return visit from the gang member. Every time the door opened, she felt her heart jump. But it was noon, and he had not come back. She went outside to take rubbish to the bin, and as she was doing so, she saw a man approach—a customer perhaps—a tall young man, dark-haired and very thin. He looked as if he were in need of a good square meal.

"We have bangers and mash," she said to him, as he hesitated before the shop.

"I have no money," he said flatly, and began to walk on.

Clare was about to let him go, but he was only a few steps away when she called: "It's all right. You don't have to pay, at least not today, if you're down on your luck."

He turned around.

"Are you sure?"

"I'm sure. Come in."

He seated himself at a table and ate mashed potatoes and a roll of bread, refusing the bangers or chops. He washed it down with a tankard of tea. Clare watched him from the back.

He really needed that meal. How horrible it must be to be hungry!

"That was awfully good of you," he said brightly when she reappeared. "I should introduce myself. I'm Edgar Murgatroyd. I used to work in the Shipyard but lost my job because of illness. I have been unsuccessful in finding another."

"You look better already," Clare said warmly. "I'm Clare Glennon, and this is my sister, Anna." Anna had appeared beside her and beamed at the new customer.

"Hallo, Miss Anna," he said with a smile and a slight bow of his head.

"I crochet lace roses," said Anna, showing him one. "Here's one for your sweetheart's hat. The first one is free."

"That's very kind of you, Miss Anna, but I don't have a sweetheart. Miss Glennon, have you been open very long?"

"Only four weeks. We came here from Devon some time ago, and needed something to do. London is a hard place to begin."

Anna, humming a tune to herself, had gone back into the kitchen.

"You're to be commended." Edgar said. "Not many women are able to stand on their own two feet."

"I have Anna to care for." Clare smiled.

"She's blessed with you. My mother is dependent upon me."

Clare did not answer. Her eyes had wandered to the window, and become troubled.

He saw her tremble. "What's the matter? Miss Glennon?"

Out the window, Clare had seen the gang member approach. Edgar turned and saw him too. But the youth passed on and did not come in.

"Are they giving you trouble?" asked Edgar.

She nodded. "They want money. Five shillings a week or there will be trouble. He threatened us." Her voice shook.

"You need a cup of tea," he remarked. "Miss Anna? Can you make your sister a cup of tea?"

"All right!" Anna came out a few minutes later carrying a tankard with care. "There you are, love," she said, setting it in front of her, and then returned to what she had been doing.

"That's the fellow they call The Cadger." Edgar said. "I knew him once. He's not good."

"What should I do?" asked Clare with desperation. "Tell the police?"

"No, not that. They'll take revenge. Tell them that you have your own bully—and then employ one."

Clare had an inspiration. "Will you do it, Mr. Murgatroyd? Will you be the guard—er—bully?"

He was surprised and also a little worried for her— she was naïve indeed! As he was, once upon a time!

"Miss Glennon, I'm very flattered you ask me, and have formed a good opinion of me, but how do you know you can trust me?"

Her reply surprised him.

"People who like Anna are always good people," she whispered to him. "I've learned that. You see my poor sister." Her eyes welled in tears.

Clare saw his eyes soften and knew she had made the correct assumption.

"I can't pay you much," she said. "But you can eat all you like here and take leftover food home. What of it? Do you want to think about it?"

"I don't have to think about it. When can I begin?"

"Now, if you haven't any pressing engagement."

"I don't. There isn't much to do in guard duty, so can I be your factotum? Run errands, and so on?"

Her eyes brightened. "Oh, that would be a great advantage! I can barely manage some of the hauling to and fro."

"So, what's my first duty, Miss Glennon?"

"Our potatoes are running low. I get them from a grower in Lambeth. Can you go for them? You'll have to walk there, and can pay for a lift coming back, there are always carts coming this way. Do you feel well enough?" she asked quickly, remembering that he was ill.

"I feel much stronger. Thank you."

"Only carry what you are able—and there's no hurry."

As he was leaving, money in his pocket and his burlap sack in hand, he turned and said:

"Miss Glennon, I can cook a bit too—nothing fancy, but grill and boil and mash. I'd be so grateful if you'd let me observe you when you're cooking, to improve myself."

"Would you really like that, Mr. Murgatroyd?"

"I would. And, you should call me Edgar."

He set off. Clare began to scour the tables. Was she a fool? Was he, and her money, gone? Though she had seen his gentle character, it didn't mean he was honest. But he would return, she thought. She looked forward to his return. She felt greatly relieved about the prospect of having a guard, a protector—a 'bully.' How much she still had to learn! He seemed to know the streets and their unsavoury inhabitants.

She also liked his kind, dark eyes and the way he moved, purposeful. *Stop, Clare,* she told herself. *Men don't like girls like you, plain, not much to look at. You don't turn heads.*

It's just as well I've decided never to get married, she thought then. *It will be just me and Anna, all our lives. We're a family. Edgar is strictly business!*

43

GOD LOVES

"**Y**ou got a job, good boy."

"Yes, Mother."

She was very interested to hear that he was a guard for a chop-house, which term she resisted using, and that all his meals would be provided. "I must visit you there," she declared, resolving that she also would get whatever was going.

"Please don't, Mother."

"Why not?" she was annoyed.

"I'm simply asking you not to," said Edgar. His mother looked down upon people who were different. And Miss Glennon would know that immediately.

"Nonsense!" she said.

The Cadger paid another visit, but Edgar dealt with him. Clare's admiration for him grew as she saw him deflect the young man's arguments and threats in a firm way, and without giving offence. But she heard that the Scarlet Swords were not about to give up. If she did not pay them protection, then something could happen to the business. It could be burgled, and everything carried off. It could go up in flames.

"I'll stay here all night, if necessary," Edgar said.

"There's no need—Mr. Grimes's hut is just a little way off, they wouldn't dare do anything."

"You don't know these people," Edgar said. "I do. I know them better than you think."

He said this in such a definite way that Clare began to wonder if he had been at their mercy at some time. However, he was not about to talk of it.

Winter was in. Everybody had coughs and colds. Edgar, who could do passable mutton chops and a fry-up, was able to keep the chop-house open when Anna became ill and Clare had to stay at home with her. What a shame that Edgar's mother could not do them a useful service like looking after Anna! But Mrs. Murgatroyd had not incurred Clare's good opinion. She had visited them and had looked askance at Anna and stepped back from her. Edgar was embarrassed and had apologised after she left.

"Where do you get your kindness from?" Clare asked. It seemed to her that if a parent was deficient in that way, then a child would be too.

"My old Nanny, and my faith," he said. "Our God is a God of love."

"Were you always interested in your faith? I mean, as a little child in Oxford?" Edgar had told her of his childhood and what had befallen his family, and Clare had told him of how she and Anna had come to be in London. They talked very easily to each other.

"No, I was not interested much, though Nanny bade me say my night prayers in her hearing. I became fervent when I was in—in prison, and I began to read the Bible. I went to prison twice. The first time, I was newly-arrived in London, only twelve years old, we were destitute, and a gang promised me money if I helped them steal from a garden. But they assaulted and robbed a man. The second time—" This was harder for him to explain. He told her the whole story, and wondered if he would have a job at the end of it. He had been such a fool to have been taken in. But there was something very straightforward and sympathetic about Clare. And she had an uncommonly good complexion for someone who lived in so much dust and smoke. Her lips looked soft and sweet—he liked them very much —she had a warm and beautiful smile. He felt he would like to kiss her. But he should not have feelings like that for his employer!

Anna still coughed and Clare was concerned about her. She lacked energy, but her smile was ever-present. She came to love Edgar almost as much as she had once loved her Papa. And he returned the devotion. He regarded Anna as his little sister. In their little world, Gullseye Ward, they had come to know many good, down-to-earth folks who were used to a variety of humankind coming and going and they did not remark Anna very much. She became everybody's little sister. She greeted many shopkeepers on her way to work, and Clare was told, more than once, that she 'had put people in a good mood with her cheeriness, the Lord bless her.'

44

CHOP-HOUSE CHRISTMAS

Christmas was Anna's Birthday, and Clare took her to church where carols were sung. She liked having the same birthday as Jesus, and over and over made Clare tell her of the morning of her birth, when she and Mary had woken up to find out that they had a new sister.

"And I thought you'd be found in our Christmas stocking," Clare always told her, to her great amusement. "We emptied them out, with me telling Mary to be careful! Then Papa sent us upstairs and there you were, in Mama's arms. You looked so tiny!"

"But why am I different, Clare?"

"Mama said you were a special baby sent by God."

It was not the first time Anna had asked this question and that was the answer that Clare always gave her.

"I don't like being different, but I do like being me. I have a happy time."

"The world is blessed with you, Anna."

Clare had decided to cook Christmas dinner in the chop-house. They had gaily decorated it the week before, and Edgar had obtained a Christmas tree. They invited him and his mother to Christmas dinner, and though there was no dinner set better than pewter to put out, Clare had borrowed a bright tablecloth. Mr. Percy had given her the gift of half a goose.

A delicious aroma filled the hut. Their guests arrived. Mrs. Murgatroyd was not there for the company, but for the feast. She had to endure one to get the other. The company was worse than she'd envisaged, for with the aroma wafting outward toward the poor houses, a few homeless orphans drifted to the door and were taken in also.

On the way home, Mrs. Murgatroyd observed to Edgar that he should look for another job.

"No, Mother," he said with infinite patience. "I'm very happy there."

"You're happy there because you're half in love with Miss Goodall."

"Their name is Glennon, Mother."

"Marriage with her is highly inadvisable, Edgar, with insanity in the family."

"Mother, it's not 'insanity'—it is a defect of birth—actually, sometimes I wish the entire world was like Anna Glennon. She spreads joy and wishes nobody ill. She treats everybody the same, I believe if she met the Queen she'd ask her how she was, same as she asks the crossing-sweeps and the beggars."

"You would have to take her on, with Miss Glennon, unless you were to convince her to put her away."

"That will never happen, Mother. Clare is devoted to her sister and wants above all things to have her with her."

"Then leave her to it. Don't marry, Edgar. Marriage is such an onerous responsibility in any case."

"You don't want me to marry at all then, Mother?"

"Oh, not for years and years."

Edgar smiled ruefully. His mother wanted all of his income and was not willing to share it with anybody.

Edgar knew he was in no position to marry. He hadn't a penny of his own.

GENTLE ANNA

T he weather continued cold, and Anna became ill again. She coughed so much that her face turned blue, alarming Clare, who found she could not breathe easy until the coughing fit was over and Anna, with a weak smile, said: "I'm all right now, Clare." She went to the druggist for a cough elixir which helped somewhat, and Clare thought that at last, she was becoming better.

With Edgar in charge at the chop-house, Clare stayed at home with her.

She sent for the doctor one day when Anna's colour was grey and she hardly had strength to get up to use the chamber pot. Her breathing was rapid.

The doctor spoke to Clare outside the door.

"It's not a hopeful case, I'm afraid. The coal dust and smoke of the City is affecting her lungs. I would tell you to take her back to Devon, but she is far too ill to travel."

Clare was stunned. She paid the doctor, saw him out the door and returned hastily to Anna.

She was sleeping peacefully. With time, and good nursing, she would recover. She would. But Anna's condition grew worse as the week wore on. She could not eat, only drank little sips, and wanted to sleep. Her breathing became more laboured. Edgar called to her daily on his way to and from the chop-house. "Everybody is asking for her," he told Clare. "They miss her and are praying for her." Still, Clare clung to the belief that her sister was not seriously ill, even when Dr. Bishop told her to expect the worst. She held off on writing to her father.

On Saturday, as darkness closed in around the Court around five o'clock, and the lamplighter had come and gone, Clare could bear the burden alone no longer. She sent for Edgar, telling him to close the chop-house and come immediately. He arrived without delay.

Weeping softly, she told him what was on her mind.

"Dr. Bishop said *again* that it was the smoke and dirt of the City. I made such a dreadful mistake bringing her here!" she said in whispered sobs, her hands gripping each other. "I thought I was saving her, but I wasn't! I will never forgive myself if—if—"

He impulsively took her in his arms. It was the first time he had done so and the impropriety of it only glided past him as a distant thought. He'd deal with that later. Clare did not pull away or make any sign that he had done wrong. "Shh. Don't say those things. She may pull through. Anna has spirit," he said.

But even Edgar could see that spirit might not be enough to save her. The only sounds were the crackling of the fire and the breathing that seemed to become more difficult and shallow every five minutes.

"What shall I do? What shall I do? Edgar, tell me what to do!" Clare was distraught.

"We can pray."

"Oh, how could I forget to pray!" Clare drew away from him and knelt by the bed, clasping her hands. Edgar got to his knees beside her. "Lord, this present moment belongs to you. I cannot think beyond it. I cannot think at all. Take care of my darling sister."

Her head fell on her breast in silence, and when she raised it, it was to say: "If God wants her with Him, Edgar, I can't fight God! Nor do I want to! He knows what's best, though it will break my heart!"

He drew her close and she wept onto his shoulder of rough, scratchy worsted, strangled sobs because she did not want Anna to hear them, if she could still hear.

Murmurs came from outside the window. "Who is there? What's going on?" Clare asked, raising her tear-streaked face.

Edgar got up and pulled the curtains back to behold a motley crowd of persons outside, nearly all from Gullseye. There was the shopkeeper who Anna greeted every morning as he put out his goods. There was the crossing-sweep she always had a cheery word for. There were Jimmy and Lucy, child beggars to whom she always gave her pennies, and who Clare regularly fed; the widow who said the sight of Anna always made her day, many neighbours from Lanyard Lane, and several warehouse hands who were regular customers.

"I'm afraid I told Mr. Grimes, and … word got around." Edgar said, embarrassed.

"It's all right. It is, really." Clare bent over her sister's head and said to her;

"Anna, darling, your friends have come to you." She gently pushed a stray hair from her forehead. Anna was unable to respond, but Clare always imagined afterwards that she saw a slight movement at the corners of her lips that was a smile.

Anna died about an hour later. Edgar went out to tell the gathering. There were lamentations and tears, and someone began to softly sing the ballad *'Gentle Annie,'* the very popular song from the United States. It was taken up by someone else, and then others, and soon the crowd was singing, heartfelt and mournful, outside in the dark under the gaslight, with a larger crowd of passers-by hastening into the Court to see what was happening, and neighbours opening their windows to lean out and listen. The constable on his beat came to see what it was all about and upon being told, shed a tear that he hoped nobody detected.

Thou wilt come no more, gentle Annie,

Like a flower thy spirit did depart.

Thou are gone, alas! like the many,

That have bloomed in the summer of my heart.

Shall we never more behold thee?

Never hear thy laughing voice again.

When the springtime comes, gentle Annie,

When the wild flowers are scattered o'er the plain.

A DIFFERENT WOMAN

"I have to let Papa know. And I will have to give him my deepest regrets that I acted as I did, because if I had not done so, Anna would still be alive." Clare buried her head in her hands.

"Stop tormenting yourself, Clare!" Edgar was growing more and more concerned. Clare was losing interest in the chop-house and was talking of going back to Devon. It was the last thing he wanted!

She wrote to her father and awaited his answer. She looked at the envelope when it came, and was afraid to open it. Would it contain bitter recriminations, harsh words? Finally she slit it open with her penknife and braced herself.

It was a letter full of love and self-blame. Her father spoke of his own torment, how he had failed them.

The load began to roll away from Clare's heart as she read on. His last words were:

'Clare, Anna was never meant to live long. Your dear mother and I thought she would pass from us before she was ten years old. Be at ease, daughter, she lived beyond what was expected for a person with her congenital defect. You made her last years happy. I wish I could say the same!'

The letter ended with an exhortation to her to return to Devon to her father, stepmother and half-brothers. He enclosed a cheque drawn on the Bank of England for fifteen pounds. She had never had so much money in her life! She'd use some of it for a beautiful headstone for Anna.

The following morning, she told Edgar about the letter. He was happy for her, but a little worried that she would leave; not only did he love Clare Glennon, but he loved his work. He, Clare and Annie had been like a little family in the Devon Chop-House. Now it was breaking up. It made him morose to think of it. Her father would keep her now; she could have an easy life and not have to earn her living. He could not, on his own, afford the rent for this premises. He saw his love, and his future drain away. But her next words raised his spirits.

"As I read the letter, exhorting me to come back, I knew I would not. I don't want to live with my stepmother. And I know she doesn't want me, so there it is, and it's not like I'll ever get married." Clare said firmly.

"I'm relieved to hear you say you'll stay, but—why do you say you won't get married?" He blushed as he spoke, his eyes alight with love.

Clare saw this and her heart did a somersault. "I—I don't know, I just never thought I would—" she couldn't finish the sentence. She did not really believe anymore that she was ill-favoured. When she looked in the mirror now, she saw a different woman. Yes, there was great sorrow there in her countenance, but her features had matured—come into their own. Her eyes seemed larger and lustrous; her high brow not the monstrosity she'd thought it to be. She wondered at the change. Was it her? Or was it the way she saw herself? She was still no beauty, she was sure, but she felt beautiful. How odd the mind was!

"Sit down, Clare, if I might give you an order in your own establishment." He took her hand. "You're in mourning, I know. I will respect it. When—if—you feel at any time you'd like to—marry—I hope it will be—to me," he finished. He felt very awkward. He had not meant to say it.

She withdrew her hand gently, and stood up. "You're the only bachelor I know!" she quipped.

"I should not have spoken. I am sorry."

"Please, don't be sorry. And I didn't mean to make light of your words. I'm happy that you feel so. But—now is not the time." Her eyes were sincere and kind.

She had told him all except that her father had sent her a great sum of money. She congratulated herself upon her wisdom, because if he knew about it, she would not know if the fifteen pounds was putting the light of love in his eyes. At least, she knew he loved her for herself. And she loved him too. Anna was her reason for coming to London, Edgar would be her reason for staying. She relied upon him. He was trustworthy and kind, and she thought about him all the time.

THE CADGER

"Why has business been so bad these last few days?" Clare wondered aloud to Edgar as he returned from the butchers on a windy day in March.

"A new place has opened and is undercutting you," was the startling reply from Edgar.

"What?"

"It's on the corner of Halley Street and Merchants. It has a portly chef in a tall white hat, there's a big bright sign, and serves eel pie. What did I often tell you?"

"That we should serve eel pie with its horrid green gravy."

"Beloved of the Cockney is his eel pie and mash potato, and even more beloved is the green liquor. Will you begin it? Eels are cheap."

At one o'clock the door opened. Mrs. Murgatroyd had come for another free meal. At least she thought they were free; but Edgar hated this and always paid, though Clare protested that he didn't need to.

"Good afternoon, Miss Glennon. Edgar, you didn't give Edie enough money for wax candles this morning, and she had to get tallow." Mrs. Murgatroyd seated herself on one of the two chairs and waited to be served. "Nobody here today," she remarked, with meaning. "I passed a new place on my way here. It looks fancy."

But just then the door opened again, and the Cadger slithered in, not coming farther than a foot inside.

"I just thought you'd like ter know," he began, his face stony, "The bloke who owns most of the properties in Gullseye is sellin' 'em to another bloke. Some toff who lives out foreign. Everything will be knocked down to make room for big blocks of housing."

Edgar and Clare were silent for a moment. "How do you know that?" Edgar asked him.

"I knows it cos I 'ave my sources, Bully."

"I've no doubt you have your sources, but how reliable are your sources?"

"I've had reason to fink 'em very reliable in the past, such as when Mr. Hally there was about to turn off fifty hands, we knew about that afore it 'appened, and we were able to set the keel of a ship in the stocks alight, to warn 'im."

"That was you? There's an innocent man in jail for that!" said Edgar very angrily.

"Hold your horses, Bully. It's not my concern that the coppers are bad at their job. Besides, I din't do it. I never said that. Now I'm doing you a favour. If these places get sold, you'll be out of business."

"I told you before, we don't own this premises." Clare said.

"You can join up with us, an' stop this, or you can go with Basher Rasher of the Scuttlers. He's on the side of the fellow who wants to buy. It's five shillings a week if you want us to work for you ter save yer business 'ere."

Clare looked at Edgar, who said: "Leave it with us for a few days, orright? We'll look into it."

The Cadger shrugged. "Don't blame me if you get burned out." He left, banging the door after him.

"What a dandy young thug!" exclaimed Mrs. Murgatroyd. "Velveteen coat!" She got up and looked out the window to get a better view of his departing back. "What did he call that other fellow? *Basher Rasher!*" She seemed very amused indeed.

"Edgar, I must go immediately to Mr. Haldane and ask him the situation with regard to selling this hut," said Clare, reaching for her cloak.

After she had left, Edgar's mother was free to speak her mind.

"Here's your chance, Edgar, to get out of all this and into something respectable."

"Mother, you don't understand about Clare. I'm in love with her."

"Oh no, Edgar. You stupid boy. She isn't in love with you. I was observing her closely. We women know these things. You're in for a big let-down. Don't come crying to me. Is there any luncheon being served here today or no?"

48

BASHER RASHER

Mrs. Murgatroyd made her way home chuckling to herself. "Basher Rasher! Basher Rasher!" People turned and stared, but she was oblivious to them, until she was suddenly accosted by a 'bloke' in a black top hat with a blue band, and a blue satin smoking jacket with frayed collar and cuffs, and brown corduroy trousers. He dangled a cigar between finger and thumb.

"Hey! What are you doing, going along sayin' my name like that?"

Mrs. Murgatroyd halted in shock at the spectacle before her, the satin smoking jacket almost touching her, the young but hard blue eyes looking at her with great suspicion.

"I didn't mean—are you—?"

"Yes, I'm Bartholomew Tarkington, Basher Rasher," he said, as a little group of giggling children gathered around. "Now can you tell me why you are going along the street saying my name aloud?"

"It's not against the law, is it?" Mrs. Murgatroyd had spirit, and nobody in a cast-off smoking jacket was going to intimidate her.

"I don't suppose it is against the law," he smirked. "But where did you hear my name? It isn't often talked of, that is, without some respect."

"Respect, is it?" Mrs. Murgatroyd's eyes roved over the comical figure. But she dared not laugh. "I respect you, Mr. Tarkington. Believe me, I do. In fact, I may wish to speak with you—in a more private setting."

She had an idea. Mr. Tarkington looked surprised. He waved the children away with a roar and they scattered in a flash of bare legs. He drew Mrs. Murgatroyd into the relative privacy of the gable end of a shop.

"Whose ma are you?" he asked. "One of the new boys? Because once they're in the Scuttler Blues, they never leave."

"I'm nobody's mother, at least, nobody you know. That isn't the matter I want to discuss with you. I have some information."

He frowned and shook his head.

"Oh, yes, about The Cadger."

"Cadger!" a long bony hand went instinctively inside the jacket, as if to meet with an indispensable prop when his rival was mentioned. Mrs. Murgatroyd was sure it was a knife, and it made her catch her breath.

"The Cadger is getting people to turn to him, against you and the 'bloke' who owns most of Gullseye. I overheard him in a business today, threatening the tenants to come to his side."

"I say, now isn't that interesting. What's your name, Missus? Because you can give me useful information and I can reward you, you know?"

"Reward?" Mrs. Murgatroyd saw a shower of gold coins fall into her lap. She would not enquire whence they came. "What kind of reward?"

"I can get something' out of pawn for you."

"I have nothing in pawn!" she laughed at the idea. But Mr Tarkington did not like to be laughed at, so she said: "I appreciate your offer all the same, Mr.

Tarkington. I do not want any reward except to get the owner of the Devon Chop-Shop, in Lanyard Lane, away from my son."

"She's a Miss Glennon, isn't she? You 'ave something against this Miss Glennon?"

"I have. I don't want my son to marry her, and she's out to get him."

"I 'ave never been asked the like before, Missus, but I'll see what I can do. Maybe I can offer myself instead, I'm free at the moment." He took off his hat and plastered his dark bear-greased hair down on his forehead.

"I am serious," Mrs. Murgatroyd said indignantly.

"But so am I," he countered.

"How do I get in touch with you, Mr. Tarkington?"

"The Old Chimneys, Tye Road. Ask for Sidney."

"Very well. You will not, I hope, forget your part of the bargain?"

"I'm on my way to Lanyard Lane now," he said, a sarcastic expression on his face as he replaced his hat.

"One more thing," Mrs. Murgatroyd was burning with curiosity. "How did you get your nickname?"

"I was four years old, my sister pestered me, so I took a rasher my mother was going to fry up and hit her with it."

Mrs. Murgatroyd thought that this was funny, very vulgar though it was. She made her way home thinking that had she been born to this kind of life, that she would have been somebody to reckon with in the neighbourhood, tough and irascible. She could hardly believe what she had done! Her life was very boring, and this activity held quite a thrill for her. She wondered what else she could find out for Basher Rasher of the Scuttler Blues. To part Edgar from Clare Glennon would be a tremendous feat!

49

THE CITY THAT DRIVES THE WORLD

iss Glennon was not attractive to Mr. Tarkington. He'd watched the hut and after a while she come out to the bin which was situated around the side. No, too thin, quiet-like and she was in mourning to boot. In any case, he was sweet on Abby Macaulay, the brassy barmaid at the Tackle That public house. There were other ways to do Mrs. Murgatroyd the favour she needed. He went away to think about it.

Edgar, on his way from the market, saw him. He knew the way the Scuttlers dressed, and his actions were suspicious. Was he spying on Clare? He decided to say nothing about it.

"Fresh eels." He laid the box on the table. "They're not alive, never fear."

"All right." Clare sat down and began to write out a sign: 'EEL PIE & MASH TONIGHT.' "I hope this attracts customers!"

"I have to go out again for a short while," Edgar said. "It concerns what we heard earlier today. I have to alert the tradespeople, assuming that it is true of course, and that The Cadger hasn't a reason to lie to us. Will you manage for a bit?"

"Of course. Mrs. Carton, three doors down, said she'd show me how to cook this. The green gravy is only parsley. That makes it sound a lot better. I'll pay her a few shillings. She needs it badly, poor woman. Thorpes have got a set of brand-new furniture and will sell their old settee for a half-crown." Clare looked up at him and smiled. It was a brave smile, and he knew that her heart was still aching for Anna. His gaze lingered with her a moment in kind regard. He wanted to stroke her hair and tell her that he was at her side at any time she needed him. But he had to allow her to find her own way.

He remembered that when he had come out of prison he had resolved never to do anybody a good turn again. Thank God he had met Clare! She brought out the best in him. He owed his position, and perhaps his life, to her act of kindness that day in extending a hand to him. She wanted nothing in return. What would he have turned out like, had he not met her? Selfish, unseeing and disinterested in others' needs? It was very possible that he could have become as selfish as his own mother.

It was about to get dark. He visited Thorpe's first and told the shopkeeper what he knew. Mr. Thorpe listened intently, his brow furrowed. "The Cadger? He'll be lyin' through his teeth. Come on now, they 'ave all sorts of swindles."

Just for a moment, Edgar wondered if he had been taken in again.

"I'm aware of that," he said then, "but it's incumbent upon us to find out the truth. Because if it is, the consequences are very serious for everybody living and trading here. For those who may be able to stay, this area will become a slum. They'll build houses with inferior material that will crumble in ten years. The poorest people will have to live in them. The roads will become open sewers."

Thorpe said nothing. They had been overheard by a woman on her way out of the shop, and the news had been relayed on the street. When Edgar emerged, he found a spirited crowd gathering around him. Thorpe followed him. Mr. Camp, a rope-maker, darted up to them.

"There was a fellow that came around here yesterday in a hansom. A swell in a top hat, said his name was Wickham. He wished to see my premises. He was *'makin' a survey for the City*, he said, and I asked to see his papers, and he said he din't have them with 'im."

"He came to me too, and I saw 'im over at Lowes. He was trying to reckon how much it would cost to knock this street, I'll bet."

"Our family 'as traded 'ere for three 'undred years!" came a cry from Mrs. Petty, who was married to a sail-maker. "How are we to begin all over again and get new customers?"

Feelings were running so high and everybody was shouting over everybody else, so Edgar proposed a meeting. They fixed it for the following night in Mr. Crossley's, the Undertaker's, for he had a large work-room.

Edgar hurried back to the Devon. There were a few customers enjoying the new item on the menu. When it was time to close, they locked the hut and he walked Clare home. As usual, the streets had their night-time walkers, watchers and revellers but nobody disturbed the couple as they went up Lanyard Lane, Merchant Street and beyond. As they approached Lydia Place, Clare's footsteps slowed and a morose silence overcame her.

"Anna is gone forever, and sometimes I can't bear it," she said.

"It's very hard," he said to her with sincerity. "I miss her too, but not as much as you, of course. When my father died, I felt as if the world had come to an end. But we have to go on."

They reached her front door, and she opened it. Edgar usually stood on the doorstep until she had unlocked the door of her room. Tonight, he followed her in. She did not seem to think it forward. She unlocked her door.

"Goodnight, Clare," he pressed her hand to convey all that was on his heart, though he thought it a very inadequate way to convey feeling.

"Goodnight, Edgar," she hesitated. "I appreciate you attending the meeting tomorrow. You're far more than a guard and a factotum. Looking out for my interests is beyond the call of duty."

"It's my privilege, Clare. Not only on your behalf but on that of the merchants as well. When I worked for the shipyard, I had a spectacular view of this ward and indeed beyond, of London, from high up on the gantry—the scaffolding. It's an amazing sight. I came to love it beyond any other place, and I've come to love the people. I understand them. Yet, I've been on the other side—the privileged side. In Oxford, I thought the traders demanding payment from my parents were unreasonable. If I hadn't been made poor, I would have turned out like my parents. Not that I like being poor!"

"You've forgiven those Londoners then, and what they did to you before?"

"There are good and bad people everywhere. I love the spirit here. Here is the city that drives the world. And yet, I detest the greed here too, the greed that forces the poor to live hand to mouth. Many have a desperate struggle. How do you feel about London?"

"Sometimes I love it too. Sometimes, I don't. It's the bad air in winter, and the smells in summer."

"What about an excursion to the country soon? Next Sunday? We'll go to Brighton. In fact, we could even go to Bolougne for the day! We'd set off from London Bridge at 7:30, and be back just before midnight. We can even go to church in Boulougne! Will you come?"

"All right!" she sounded brighter, looking forward to it. "What will your mother say to it?"

"My mother will be quite all right for a day by herself."

"It's settled, then!" Clare suddenly leaned forward and kissed him on the cheek. "Goodnight," she said quickly, to cover her embarrassment.

She shut her door behind her. She lit the lamp. It usually made her very dejected to see Anna's workbag on the table, with the rose she had been working on still out, folded around the hook. Her Sunday bonnet rested on a chair. She had given the rest of her clothes away but could not bear to part with that, though it was only a simple straw with a wreath of silk and lace flowers and a green ribbon. Her doll, Lily, sat on the chair. Tonight, Clare took up the hook and thread and put them back in the work bag. The bonnet—she would give it to Mrs. Kelly for her daughter Sally. As for Lily, she knew a little girl in Lanyard Lane who had no doll—she knew what Annie would wish her to do ...

An excursion to Bolougne on Sunday next!

As Edgar began the walk home, he said to himself that he wouldn't wash his face for a month. He leaped and punched the air. Bolougne! He'd pawn the Roman coin to pay for it.

50

THE OLD CHIMNEYS

Mrs. Murgatroyd made ready to go to the Old Chimneys in Tye Street. She felt impatient. Edgar had told her he was going on an Excursion on Sunday and she was quite angry, for he was taking Miss Glennon!

Normally, Mrs. Murgatroyd would not be seen dead in a place like the Old Chimneys. It was a place for prostitutes and drunkards. But she could not sit and do nothing. She had little to do except mull over Edgar and Miss Glennon, and she could bear the suspense no longer. The news of the excursion was burning a hole in her brain. She set off at a smart pace, and reached it twenty minutes later. A squalid, run-down place. She had not expected better.

She pushed open the door and saw that she was in semi-darkness, but she made out figures—women as well as men, thank goodness, though a very low kind of woman, she was sure—in the long room reeking of beer and tobacco. She saw a counter and leaning across it, asked the barman for 'Sid,' in a whisper.

"Halloo, Sid!" the barman called across to a dark cavern, and a burly shape emerged from it.

"I'm Sid. What do you want?"

"I have a message for Mr. Tarkington."

"The Basher Rasher? He's here. Rasher! She's for you," he roared, causing Mrs Murgatroyd to become embarrassed and everybody else to snigger.

She was beckoned to enter the cavern, a secluded snug where three men sat. The Basher got rid of the others, and before he could say anything, she asked him how he succeeded with Miss Glennon.

"Oh, I din't go fer her. She's not my type. 'Ave you got anything for me?"

"Not until you get rid of Miss Glennon."

"Get rid of her, is it? You surely don't mean—" he dragged his finger across his throat. "Cos that would be very expensive."

"Oh goodness no. Not that. Can't you tell her that whoever you're working for is something in Public Health and is going to shut her down?"

"Aw no. That's too tame for me. She wouldn't believe it anyway. Wickham in the Government! He's only a steward for some old fellow who lives abroad. Longnecker—no, Longfellow."

It was as well that Mrs. Murgatroyd was in semi-darkness, for her eyes would have betrayed her surprise. *Longfellow!* Was it—could it be possibly be Uncle Evelyn? Her heart thumped fast. This was a marvel!

"And this old fellow—does he ever come back to England?"

"I don't think so."

"Doesn't he have any family?"

"No, he's a bachelor, I think. Not that I care. Why are we talking of 'im anyway? It's Wickham who concerns us, innit."

When Edgar walked Clare home that night, he told her of what occurred at the meeting, including the fact that he had been elected Chairman of the committee they had formed to fight Mr. Wickham. He was only an agent but they'd make it difficult for him. Clare was very happy to hear it and very proud of him. The committee intended to write a letter to their MP and to the newspapers to try to win support. They'd stage demonstrations and protests, and if they could not stop the sale they would at least try to stop demolition.

"I'm looking forward to Sunday," she said before they parted. She turned her face up to his and drew a little closer; he needed no encouragement—he took her in his arms and they kissed.

Edgar was very happy on the way home. He loved Clare with all his heart. While he did not have the money he needed to marry, Clare's business could make it possible. He would work as hard as he could for her, for he could make it a success. The Devon Chop-House could expand … they could work together … he could have a happy life by the side of the woman he loved and trusted.

Clare let herself into her room and lit the lamp, her heart aglow with delight. She still felt Edgar's kiss upon her lips. There would be many, many more! As soon as she was in half-mourning, she hoped they would marry and begin a new and happy life —together.

52

WALK-OUT

Edgar reached home to find his mother still up. She was in a wonderful mood as she made him a cup of tea.

"I have such news," she began. "My uncle—Uncle Evelyn Longfellow—is none other than the man who wishes to buy the properties in Gullseye Ward!"

He was astonished. "That can't be true, Mother. Where did you get such an idea?"

"I have been informed by a well-wisher, Edgar," she said. "And I have no doubt that if you attend to your great-uncle's interests, you will be richly rewarded! What do you think of that? Is it not very good news? You must go and present yourself to his agent, a Mr. Wickham, and offer to work on his behalf in bringing the tenants into line. Family duty, Edgar.

Do not make any objection—I won't have it. This is the best thing that has happened to us in a decade. He will notice us. He will befriend us. We will be rich again!"

Edgar was dumbfounded. "I still think you're mistaken, Mother," he said at last, "It's not our uncle. It cannot be. I don't want you to hope. And even if it is our Uncle Evelyn, I'm not going to be a turncoat. My sentiments lie in the other direction, with Clare and the other tenants, for I see the injustice being done to them."

"Edgar!" she shrieked. "You cannot be so unfeeling, so stubborn, so horrible! Have you forgotten what it was like to have a nice place to live and good boots on your feet, and money? If you can't think of yourself, think of me! I'm sick of poverty! What you bring home for me to live on is a pittance! How can I, a lady, live on that?"

She raged on and on, and finally Edgar could not take it anymore. He got up and went to a little cupboard, took an old carpet bag from it, stuffed his belongings inside, put his boots on again, took his coat and hat and walked toward the door. All the time, his mother was following him about and abusing him loudly.

"Where are you going?" she shrieked now. "Come back and listen to me!"

"I've had enough. I'm not coming back," he said, with determination. "Why should I wait around here and be the butt of your frustrations? I'll continue to support you but I'm not coming back."

He felt more wounded than angry. Her words stung. He worked hard for her, she took nearly everything he earned, and wasted it. He was feeling bitter. It was a cold night. He walked until he was in Lanyard Lane. It was dark and several gas lamps were broken. He found a patch of waste ground beside a wall and lay upon it. A dog came up and sniffed him. A few drunken sailors passed by without seeing him. A baby cried in a house nearby.

"She's on her own now," he said to himself with bitterness. "I will never live with her again. I've had enough!"

53

L STANDS FOR …

Edgar drifted off to sleep at some point during the night, and awoke very cold. He got up and did some exercises and then proceeded to a lodging house where he was admitted and had the use of a basin of water for washing and shaving. He devoured a piece of bread and a cup of tea there and set off. He had to find out today if what his mother had said was true, and the only way to do that was to find this man Wickham.

He'd have to skip work. He had no pencil or paper to write Clare a note, so he had to wait until she came, to see her. He did not have keys, so he waited outside. Usually he did not come until later.

"You're here already," he heard Clare say, cheerily, the memory of last night perhaps in her mind. He hoped so! At least she did not notice anything amiss with him. He greeted her warmly, and their eyes locked for a moment.

"I hope you don't mind, Clare. I have an urgent errand that has to be run this morning. It came up quite suddenly. I'm asking you for a few hours off."

"Of course," she answered fondly as she put the key in the lock. "You've been doing so much for me lately, I'm glad to return the compliment."

People were about, so they could not exchange a kiss or hold hands, so they shared a long, loving glance.

"Are you all right?" she asked him suddenly.

"I'm fine," he lied. "This business about the properties is a bit worrisome, but I'm looking forward to Sunday."

"As I am," she smiled at him tenderly.

Clare entered the hut, her heart light as summer even though there was a stiff wind this morning.

A letter had been slipped under the door and she picked it up, wondering what it could be. Nothing could have prepared her for the content.

Miss Glennon.

Mr. Murgatroyd is not who he seems to be. He is working against you. He is the great nephew of your enemy, Mr. Longfellow, whose agent Mr. Wickham is. He is a spy. He stands to gain greatly from the sale of the properties in Gullseye Ward. Ask Mr. Edgar L. Murgatroyd what the L stands for!

A Friend

Clare read the note over and over, at first not comprehending. It seemed an astounding allegation. It could not be. An anonymous letter should be discarded. Somebody had just done a very, very spiteful thing! Who?

And yet, suspicion snaked into her mind in spite of herself. He had gone to prison—twice. Was that a matter that she should have given more consideration to? She'd believed him utterly, every word. She still did!

No, it was just a spiteful letter. Someone did not want her to marry Edgar. It was all a lie; how could Mr. Longfellow allow Mrs. Murgatroyd to live in poverty in Estella Court, and how could Edgar come to such as pass as to be starving, as he had been when they met?

What did the L stand for? Had this 'errand' something to do with the meeting of last night, had he gone to report the proceedings to Wickham?

She made up her mind very quickly indeed to follow him. Turning the sign 'closed' outward, she set off smartly, keeping him in sight.

BETRAYAL

The morning was very windy. Shop signs creaked and squeaked every time a gust hit them, and shopmen tied down outdoor displays. Early daffodils in the gardens bent almost horizontal and small branches tore from the trees and whirled about Edgar's path. He wrapped his muffler up about his face and pulled his hat down. He felt a cold coming on, no doubt because of his night in the outdoors.

He knew where Wickham's office was to be found. Mr. Thorpe had pressed it upon him last night, asking him to write a stiff letter. The office was in The Strand, not a long walk, but the wind this morning was cruel. He reflected that there would have been many disappointed day labourers at the docks this morning as the ships would not have been able to dock. The wind decided whether a family would eat or not!

He did not know that Clare was following him closely behind. She kept to the shadows in case he looked around. As they reached the commercial area of the city her heart began to sink. Here were offices of all sorts, law, estate and property, with names like Currier & Sons; Landon, Bridges & Smiley on proud brass plaques, good carriages, and respectably dressed men in greatcoats and top hats coming and going.

She saw that Edgar halted before one of these buildings before mounting the steps and going through the open door. She advanced, not wanting to know and yet telling herself that she had to know. She reached the building and read the shining, embellished plaque:

Messrs Bright & Wickham,
Land Surveying & Conveyancing.

It was true, then. Joy drained from her; the morning, though the sun was now shining bravely, seemed to have grown darker. Last night had only been a cruel joke. She felt like a stupid clown. Edgar was playing her, using her business as a base from which to infiltrate the tenants of Lanyard Lane and Merchant Street and beyond. She felt chilled and bitter as she turned and walked off back the way she had come. How could he? And she was so recently bereaved too? She reached Lanyard Lane and later did not remember her journey back. She wondered what to say to Edgar when he appeared. He'd be happy and in good humour and expect the same of her.

He was in for a shock.

E dgar requested an interview with Mr. Wickham and was bidden to wait for a time. The ante-room was quiet and serene but for the scratching of the clerk's pen as he wrote careful notes into a ledger.

Edgar remembered with a mixture of bitterness and amusement the morning in Oxford that he had come down to breakfast thinking that his Uncle Evelyn was dead, and how his parents had hastened—rather too much—to disabuse him of the notion that they had ever wished him gone. The memory made him smile. What had become of his mother since then? She had been unable to adapt to her reduced circumstances and had consequently become very unhappy, shrewish and selfish. But he would not think of his mother. He would fill his heart and mind with Clare, her gentle personality, her willingness to knuckle down and work for her living, her generous heart.

But now that he was in the calm light of day, he understood somewhat his mother's frustration with a relative who had riches in plenty while she, a widow, lived in penury. It did not seem fair. It was incumbent upon him, a grown-up son, to do what he could for her, at least. Mr. Wickham did not know who he, Edgar, was—and would not connect him at all with Lanyard Lane. Edgar decided he could accomplish two things—find out if Mr. Wickham was in fact acting on behalf of his Uncle Evelyn, and if so—to try to assist his mother.

If it really was his uncle, then an appeal to him directly, from him, about Gullseye would be more beneficial than approaching his agent. There would be no need to mention Gullseye to Wickham at all this morning.

A man came out of the inner office, pulling on his gloves and bidding goodbye to the clerk, who motioned Edgar through.

"Mr. Murgatroyd, what can I do for you?" Mr. Wickham had taken a quick survey of the inferior suit of clothes on his visitor and did not bother to get up.

Edgar said his piece. Was he working for a gentleman named Mr. Evelyn Longfellow?

"It's no secret that I represent him, certainly." In response to Edward's probings, he declared that "he was quite elderly, over ninety, a bachelor," and that "yes, he lived on the continent, for his health," and "His family was originally from Oxford shire."

"Is it possible to have his address?" Edward asked.

"Why should you need his address? Anything you have to say to Mr. Longfellow, *if* you have anything to say,"—a glance again at his inferior garb—"can be relayed though me. Were you a part of his household at one time? The gardener's boy perhaps?"

"Not at all. I am related to him," Edgar said. "My mother is his niece. There was some distance put between them in the past—it was well before I was born. My mother would like to renew the contact."

"I see," Mr. Wickham at last asked him to be seated. "I shall make a representation to Mr. Longfellow to see if he wishes to renew the connection," he said. "Where might I reach you?"

"You may reach my mother directly at—" Edgar gave the address. He thought it better. Allow his mother to present herself as a woman alone, and Uncle might be all the more moved to assist her. It was a pity he did not send his mother here for herself!

The clerk entered then.

"Mr. Thorpe to see you, sir," he said testily.

"Very well, very well. And don't take that tone with me, Gibbons. Tell Thorpe I shall meet him in Hunter's Hotel in an hour."

"Yes, sir."

Thorpe? Edgar wondered—surely not—Thorpe was a common name. He made a little more conversation, though it was unwelcome to Mr. Wickham, admiring the painting upon the wall, remembering a painter cousin who worked in watercolours—surely Thorpe was gone by now, and he bid goodbye to Mr. Wickham, and as he passed the clerk outside he was pleased to see a driving shower of rain outside. A perfect excuse to linger a little longer.

"I bet yours is not an easy job," he offered Mr. Gibbons.

Scratch, scratch went the pen. "No, it's not. Some days are better than others, though."

"I hope he pays you well for all you have to put up with," was Edgar's next inducement.

The scratching ceased. "No, he doesn't. I can't tell you what I have to put up with here," he said in an angry whisper.

"I deduced that Mr. Thorpe is not your favourite client?"

"That crook! He's going to be the means of this office shutting down."

"How so?" Edgar pried. "It looks so well-run, and Mr. Wickham looks like he knows what he's about."

"I should say no more. But this Thorpe fellow, from around Gullseye. He's in cahoots with a gang and I suspect something's up. I should say no more. Good day to you, sir." The scratching began in earnest again.

Edgar found Hunters, walked around to the alley at the back and saw a back door open. He went in, his muffler over his face, saw Thorpe waiting in a corner with his eye on the front door, and took a table with his back to him. A short time later, as he nursed a pint of ale, out of the corner of his eye, he saw Wickham come in. He slipped off his outer coat so that he would not be recognised.

The men spoke in low tones, but Edgar heard enough. *Nip the protests in the bud ... raze Gullseye to the ground ... present wind will favour us ... before ten, no loss of life—I'm no murderer. Make sure he understands ...*

So Gullseye was to burn. 'He' was Basher Rasher, obviously. Edgar had to go to the Police. He was not fond of them, as they held bitter memories for him, but there was no alternative.

It ran into his head at one point that Clare would wonder where he was; it was busy now at the Devon. But when he told her, she would understand.

He hoped with all of his heart that his mother would not inform her of the Longfellow connection before he did so.

THE QUARREL

C lare's heart was heavy as she prepared the lunches for the hungry men who would be by later. She was very busy, she'd got a late start, and there was no mutton today, as she had forgotten it. It was Edgar's duty in any case to get the viands in the morning. She found it hard to concentrate on what she was doing. The food she served was not as good as the patrons had come to expect, and there were grumblings—the sausages were burned, the potatoes too mushy.

The lunch customers had left; she had the dishes washed and almost dried before she saw him return. It was past three o'clock. He came straight to the kitchen, and she did not turn or greet him.

"I'm sorry, Clare. I was delayed. I will tell you all about it—" He picked up a cloth and began to dry the remaining dishes. She snatched the cloth out of his hands.

"Clare, what's the matter? I can explain why I was late—please don't be upset."

"Are you on our side or, are you not?" She demanded of him. She pulled the note from her pocket and thrust it at him.

"I was afraid of this," he groaned when he had read it.

"Were you? Afraid you'd be found out?"

"I have nothing to hide, Clare."

"Miss Glennon to you."

There was a silence.

"I think you had better leave." Clare went to the till and took out ten shillings. "There's two weeks wages. Go now, Mr. Murgatroyd, and don't come back."

"Clare—you can't mean this—"

"I believed you, every word you said, about how you were framed—twice—I should have known better!

You yourself told me I was too trusting! You took me for a fool!"

This was a very unkind cut and he felt an icy deluge drench his heart. Then he became angry. He'd spent the night in the open, he had a sore throat, he felt feverish, and the ugly quarrel with his mother the evening before was still resonating in his ears—now Clare had turned against him!

"Will you hear me?" he demanded. She turned away. "You don't trust me, is that it? I shall go, then." He left, spurning his wages, and Clare sat at a table after he had left, and burst into tears.

SPARKS FLY

T hat evening, Clare walked home alone, her head down, not speaking to anybody, ignoring the lewd calls from sailors and approaches from drunks. As she neared her house, she thought she heard a footstep behind her. Frightened, she turned suddenly. Edgar was a little way off, watching her. Under the streetlamp, he had a guilty look, and he merely waved his hand once and turned away.

Following her! Why? To make sure she got home safely! In her room, she leaned her back against the shut door and wept again. She had no heart for anything now, nothing at all. The Devon had lost its charm. Without Anna, and now without Edgar, the hut was unbearable. Before, she had pride and joy in it. Now, it would be bitter to be there.

It was difficult to drag herself out of bed the following day—if she could but have stayed unconscious of pain for just a little more time! But she got up and dressed. The day stretched ahead of her, and she knew it would be unhappy and miserable. How much longer could she stand it? She still had her father's money—most of it. She could go anywhere she liked away from the memories. But there was nowhere she wished to go!

She trudged to Lanyard Lane. She was late, and finally hurried her steps, knowing she'd have a great deal of work to do today. As she neared Merchant Street she saw wisps of smoke over the rooftops and a smell of burning about. She found a little knot of people on Lanyard Lane.

"What happened?" she cried.

"There were fires last night!"

"We don't know where it started, but sparks and embers came on the wind. The police and fire engines were 'ere within a few minutes," said Mrs. Carton, holding her little girl in her arms. Clutched in little Julie's arms was Lily, and Clare felt her mood change for a moment from sorrow to tenderness.

"A few minutes! That's astonishing!"

"I'd better check my hut isn't ruined," Clare ran to the end of Lanyard Lane. Mr. Grimes saw her and came to her immediately.

"There's great damage, I'm afeard."

"Oh no." Clare immediately thought of the Cadger and his threats. Was it him?

"Where's Mr. Murgatroyd today?" Grimes asked. "He's usually here by now, you are late."

"He doesn't work here anymore," she said, biting her lip. Mr. Grimes looked at her and shook his head. "Oh dear, a lover's quarrel?" he said then. The women had followed her down and were listening— Mrs. Carton, Mrs. Murphy and others, so she said nothing.

The hut was uninhabitable. The kitchen roof was gone, and the roof of the eating area looked charred and shaky. The floors and walls were drenched with the water used to put the fire out.

"Take all this food away," Clare said to the women. "This place is finished. There's nothing left for me here."

"You wouldn't be giving a certain person her way now, would you?" demanded Mrs. Murphy, her chin jutted forward, her hand on her hips. "We know his

Ma wants you out and off. Do you love him, or don't you love him?"

Clare had no answer but had to smile in spite of herself. How did these women know so much about her? They must have little else to do but gossip! How could she explain to them that Edgar was working against them? She could not. It made her ill to think he had anything to do with the fire.

Mr. Wickham was in no humour for another enquirer about Mr. Longfellow. He had opened the newspaper expecting to see columns of news about the great fire in Gullseye Ward which had destroyed much of the area, and only dreaded to see loss of life, for that would make him feel guilty. Thorpe was to receive one hundred pounds compensation for being burned out. A fire destroying most of Gullseye would serve Mr. Longfellow's cause greatly, for it would force the tenants to give up and disperse. Why a fellow with one foot in the grave wanted Gullseye was beyond his comprehension, but it was not for him to question. Longfellow had no need to know of course, what methods were being employed to effect the sale.

But there was no mention of any fire! What had happened? What had gone wrong? Now, he had this woman in front of him who had pushed her way past Gibbons to see him. A *'distressed gentlewoman'* she called herself.

"But I had an enquiry about Mr. Longfellow yesterday from your son Mr. Edgar," he said, barely keeping his patience. She was still a handsome woman and if she were not so annoying, he could admire her. She'd given him a long story about how through no fault of her own, she had become poor and needy, and she was certain that if her uncle knew of it—he would not allow her to linger in this state.

"Edgar came? That was good of him, but a letter is too slow. You must use modern methods. I demand you send a telegraph. I will wait here until you do it."

He did not know what to do. No wonder her husband had dropped dead after breakfast. *He* would not have waited to have eaten first.

"Write this—URGENT MARIE'S GIRL AIDAH IN DEEP DISTRESS—STOP—MUST HAVE RELIEF— STOP—HUNGRY   HOMELESS—STOP—SON EDGAR AS USELESS AS HIS FATHER—STOP."

"You cannot mean me to send the last sentence," Wickham said with weariness.

"Leave it in, he did not take to my husband, and was against the marriage forced upon me."

"Is there any end to your misfortunes, Mrs. Murgatroyd?" Wickham said with more weariness.

"I am making an end to them," she replied. "By this day's end, I expect you will have orders to house me, and perhaps in his own house in Knightsbridge."

59

URGENT WORK!

The Metropolitan Police had increased their men on the beat and had the fire brigade ready. But they declined to arrest Thorpe or Wickham on suspicion of something they *might* do. Edgar was relieved that little damage had been done, none to life, and little enough to property, as far as he knew.

He'd best try to forget Clare. She had not given him a chance to explain himself. Perhaps she did not love him—his mother had told him so. Trust was very important, and she did not trust him.

.   .   .

He found lodging—how he hated derelict lodgings! Filth and smells. They were places for outcasts—opium addicts, drunkards, men and boys disabled in body or mind, those cast by the wayside, and many by circumstances outside of their control. He was shown to a narrow, stinking mattress and laid his head down. He was very ill. He could do no more today, his head was splitting, and he felt as weak as a kitten. He did not even have medicine. But he tossed and turned, unable to rest, and not just because of the scratchy straw. He had urgent work to do! He had to expose Wickham and Thorpe! He rose again, and his head throbbing, went out on the street.

60

FISTS UP!

"Clare! Is it really you?" The woman stopped her on the street. As there was still a wicked wind, her head was covered by the warm hood of her cloak and a muffler covered half of her face. But Clare recognised the voice of Miss Davey.

"Is it really *you*?" Clare said, in a happy tone. "I thought you were gone from us forever!"

They were in Lanyard Lane on the corner of Merchant Street. Clare was making her way home. She had nothing else to do.

"I came back. I'm living here again, but in a good boarding house, in Merborough St. Where's Anna?"

Clare told her the bad news. Caroline wept. "Let us have some tea," Clare said, taking her by the arm. "There's a tea-house very near."

"My brother and sister-in-law were very kind," Caroline told her as they sipped tea. "But they had no idea how I had changed, and everything I had seen of the world, especially of the poor, was of little interest to them. I became unhappy. I decided to return. My brother pays my keep, and I'll get involved in charity work. But what of you?"

Clare told her about her business, and of its recent failure.

"Did you not have anybody to help you with this?"

"There was a young man—but he betrayed me." As Clare talked on and on, Miss Davey interrupted her.

"You speak of Mr. Edgar Murgatroyd!" she exclaimed. "Clare, I have known him since he was twelve years old! I have personal knowledge of his confinements to prison, and he told you the truth!"

"But the note—and—I saw him go into Wickham's office!"

"Did he not give you any explanation?"

"I dismissed him most cruelly, I never gave him a chance to explain," she said, feeling wretched.

"Oh Clare. I feel sure he is innocent. He's noble and high-minded. He must have been on another business."

"I have to find him, Miss Davey!" she got up quickly, insisted on paying the bill, and went outside.

"Miss Glennon!" Mrs. Carton was running toward her, her skirts flying. "Thank God I've found you!"

"What is it?" she asked in alarm.

"Mr. Thorpe and your young man! Come quickly!"

The women picked up their hems and ran. There was a large crowd gathering in Lanyard Lane around two men.

"You're a traitor!" Edgar was shouting. "You're with Wickham in all this! I heard you plot the fire!" Edgar's colour was heightened, and his body swayed.

"You drunken fool!" was Thorpe's response. "You're ridiculous!"

"You were fool enough to provide me with his address, and so I went there," Edgar shouted then. He seemed to stumble. Clare looked on in deep astonishment and concern—Edgar was a very light drinker—had she driven him to inebriation?

"You're stark raving mad!" Thorpe said, taking off his jacket. "Put up your fists, we'll settle this!"

"Hey-day, Thorpe," said Mr. Carton, advancing. He was a day labourer who worked sporadically. "You've 'ad money to throw around lately, where'd you get it?"

"Carton's right!" Edgar said. He had his fists up now, and the two men lunged, but Carton intervened. Edgar fell to the ground. Clare ran to him.

"Drunkard!" Thorpe said, drawing back his leg in readiness to kick him, but Clare flung herself on top of Edgar and got the kick instead to her ribs. Thorpe was set upon and removed by Carton and several other men, while the women dropped to tend to the pair. Clare ignored the stabs of burning pain in her side as she noticed Edgar's face flushed and his eyes red and glazed. She placed her hand on his brow.

"He's burning up with fever!"

COMING TO

W hen Edgar awoke, he became aware that a young woman was by his side. He saw her get up, hold her side for a moment, and call to somebody outside.

"He's awake! He will live!"

Live? Edgar did not know what she was talking about. He clutched at the sheets, not comprehending. They were fine, soft sheets. He was in a room—thick velvet curtains about his bed— where was he? What had happened to him?

The girl was back. She looked distraught.

"Oh Edgar, can you forgive me?" she asked, agonisingly. "I so misjudged you! I didn't allow you to explain! I've told myself over and over that I was horrid to you!" Tears dripped down her cheek. "You see, I followed you and saw you go into Wickham's office—oh dear—you don't know me, do you? And you can't comprehend what I'm saying! Papa!"

What was this? Why was this girl calling her Papa? A man came in and took his pulse.

"Leave him be, Clare. He'll be better soon. Draw the curtains and allow him to sleep."

He awoke again some time later—was it hours, or days?—and found the girl there again. This time, he recognised her.

"Clare."

"Oh Edgar, I thought you were going to die! I would never have forgiven myself!"

"Why? What happened? Where am I, Clare?"

"You're in a boarding house in Merborough Street."

"That's a swanky place! I can't afford—"

"It's all right," she soothed. "Don't worry about money."

"How long have I been here?"

"Ten days."

"May I have a drink of water?"

She raised his head tenderly and put a cup to his lips.

"Thank you. You're a good nurse."

"Clare!" a male voice drifted in. "Let him be. You need to get some sleep!"

"That's Papa. I sent for him to look after you. Your mother is here too."

"My boy!" Mrs. Murgatroyd elbowed Clare out of the way. "How dare you go out into the night and get your death!"

Events were coming back to him. But he did not want to be scolded, so after saying: "Oh, Mother," he shut his eyes and pretended sleep.

"Dear boy! May I tell him, Doctor Glennon?"

"No. Absolutely not. It's too soon."

Edgar's memory returned quickly—he remembered that Clare had taken a vicious kick meant for him, and this unselfish act completely banished the hurt her words had caused him. He was concerned that she was injured—she moved very gingerly.

"Miss Davey made me see a doctor. My rib cracked or something. I'll be fine. Don't worry." She assured him. "And Thorpe is in jail."

"You know Miss Davey!" he said.

"She it was insisted you be brought here—she has rooms upstairs. She's one of the bravest women I know—but I shall tell you about that another time."

Three days later, Dr. Glennon gave Mrs. Murgatroyd permission to speak to her son of the matter she found so difficult to keep from him.

"Uncle Evelyn is dead." she announced, having the grace to try to at least look sorrowful for a moment. "He died a week ago, and you inherit all."

"I see," Edgar said without emotion.

"What's the matter with you? You can have an easy life now, and provide for me! I have borrowed money on the expectation of it, and I now have a suite at Claridge's and my own maid."

Edgar felt unmoved by the news that he was rich now. As he recovered, he remembered the time they had come to London, his sense of awe and adventure giving way very soon to hunger and cold. He remembered seeing the small boys under the dark, damp arches, and later, being trapped in a cold grey prison, and later still the desperate scramble for a day's work at the docks, the hunger and stomach pains. He felt haunted. His mother loved money and he almost despised it, until it occurred to him in a sudden flash, a moment of epiphany, that *if* the sale of Gullseye had gone through, that as well as inheriting his uncle's money, he was now the owner and principal landlord of most of Gullseye Ward. He had to find out! The following day, he had his answer. The sale had indeed gone through in the days before his uncle had died.

"Good gracious," Edgar said to Clare the following day. "I now have it in my power to improve the district, to create employment, to do all sorts of beneficial things. I must get up soon, there's such a lot to be done! For if the people want to stay in their homes, I must improve them! The buildings are timber, hundreds of years old!"

"And build a nice park," Clare said eagerly, "with green lawns, and shrubberies and flower beds! For families, locked at night, off-limits to drunkards and opium addicts and the like."

"Did you think I was drunk that day I took Thorpe on? I went to his house and practically dragged him outside. I was delirious with fever, and had one thing on my mind, getting that fellow to own up!"

One day Clare and her father went to Anna's grave in St. Mary's Cemetery. Her father knelt there and wept copious tears. He was still filled with self-reproach, but Clare said:

"Papa, you must forgive yourself. She would want you to."

"But, do you? Do you forgive me?"

"Of course, I do, Papa."

It was true that she held no grudge. It was pointless to do so. Grudges were like small doses of poison one took from time to time, preventing love from flourishing and maturing. Her father had a miserable time at home, she knew. She pitied him.

Before Dr. Glennon returned to Devonshire, Edgar asked him for Clare's hand in marriage and it was gladly given. The couple were married soon after in St. Mary's Church, and moved into the house in Knightsbridge. Clare had already examined it from top to bottom and been delighted to find a roomy kitchen, though somewhat dark and old-fashioned. She planned to install better lighting, a large modern stove, have water piped in and the latest in utensils.

The people of Gullseye wanted something more of Edgar. They wanted him to stand for election to Parliament. He obliged, surprised himself by making good, forceful speeches against his opponent, and was successful in winning the other landowners around, all of whom were voters, mostly by Clare's idea of a spacious park that would make the area more attractive and worth more in the future. His tenants were very keen on improving their homes, and Edgar was generous in providing the finances needed. He employed many poor men in the district to do the work. In the middle of the work, under the disused warehouse, was found an old Roman street. Edgar was wildly excited. Under the stones of a villa was a box of ancient coins and parchments. Other artefacts were found and antiquaries descended upon Gullseye, searching for more sites.

Had Uncle Evelyn known of this? Is that why he had wanted to buy up the area? Perhaps he would not have put up housing after all. His reasons would never be known.

As the wife of an M.P. Clare now had plenty of opportunities to improve her own culinary skills, for they had to entertain people who were used to the best cuisine. She employed a French chef for a year to teach her and afterward made sure to employ young cooks she could train in her own way, and who tolerated their mistress in the kitchen! She also had the joy of welcoming her Aunt Susanna and Captain Hammond who were returning to England for good. They spoke of their dear ones in Heaven, including Doris, who had also entered Glory. But there was new life to bring them back to the present —Clare's lively little cousins, and her own new daughter she named Anna Mary.

Mrs. Murgatroyd chose to return to Oxford, where she lived in a fine house with six servants, kept a carriage and told everybody she always knew her son would be a Member of Parliament.

Thank you so much for reading. We hope you really enjoyed the story. Please consider leaving a positive review on Amazon if you did.

WOULD YOU LIKE FREE BOOKS EVERY WEEK FROM PUREREAD?

Click Here and sign up to receive PureRead updates so we can send them to you each and every week.

Much love, and thanks again,

Your Friends at PureRead

SIGN UP TO RECEIVE FREE BOOKS
EVERY WEEK

CLICK HERE >> **PureRead.com/free**

Printed in Great Britain
by Amazon

51983357R00187